The League of the Dream Hunters

Naysan A. Albaytar

Ukiyoto Publishing

All global publishing rights are held by

Ukiyoto Publishing

Published in 2024

Content Copyright © Naysan A. Albaytar

ISBN 9789364942331

All rights reserved.
No part of this publication may be reproduced, transmitted, or stored in a retrieval system, in any form by any means, electronic, mechanical, photocopying, recording or otherwise, without the prior permission of the publisher.

The moral rights of the author have been asserted.

This is a work of fiction. Names, characters, businesses, places, events, locales, and incidents are either the products of the author's imagination or used in a fictitious manner. Any resemblance to actual persons, living or dead, or actual events is purely coincidental.

This book is sold subject to the condition that it shall not by way of trade or otherwise, be lent, resold, hired out or otherwise circulated, without the publisher's prior consent, in any form of binding or cover other than that in which it is published.

www.ukiyoto.com

Other Books by Naysan Albaytar

Remembering Pandan: A Farmer's Life and Other Stories, a memoir

All the Life Around Us, a collection of short stories

To all the aspiring writers I've met in my journey…
The world awaits your stories.

PROLOGUE

"Find Abe," her mother's soft voice wavered, but it was clear. "Find him, and you will find the dream."

Her hands reached out to take his, and bright colors emanated from her fingers as soon as she touched his wrists—green and yellow and red dancing around the tips. He felt his hands growing warm at the touch of his mother's, and the veins on his wrists started to glow faintly with the same colors.

"You must find your brother," her grasp of his hands tightened, and he felt his heartbeat quicken as he remembered Abe. "You must find him."

This last statement, she uttered much softer as the colors in her fingers grew lighter and her grasp of his hands grew weaker, the color draining from her beautiful face.

Alec watched his own hands and wrists, his mother's hands now gone. He stared at the tiny veins that ran along towards his palms, watched as the colors pulsed lightly before they slowly disappeared, the warmth going away with them.

He blinked, and after that split second of darkness, he found himself in his parents' bedroom. He looked at the bed, its sheets wine red, a metallic smell pervading the air. His parents laid there, all colors around them gone. They were black figures in a red sea, so dark it was difficult to distinguish where his mother's body started and his father's body began.

He felt, more than seen, his father holding his mother close to him, their hands intertwined. He squinted his eyes, trying to look closer as he felt a feeling of desperation in the tingling in his fingers. He searched for the colors that have always followed every flick, every movement of his mother's fingers.

Those colors were special, because only his mother had them. She would cook in the kitchen, and Alec would watch, fascinated, as the colors danced around her hands. Every movement as she chopped garlic and onions, sliced cucumbers, peeled potatoes, everything was a show that created colors coming together and drawing apart, forming and unforming, dancing in circles or flying in sparks every time she flicked her fingers or clapped her hands, sometimes unintentionally and sometimes intentionally just to amuse him, especially when he was still a child.

Even more special than all of that, only he could see them, the colors around his mother's fingers. Not his father nor his older brother could see them, but he could. And it became something special that he shared with her.

But the colors were all gone. They have disappeared. They must have drowned somewhere in that dark red pool, and in place of the colors was the feeling of guilt that had settled at the pit of his stomach since that day, one he had learned to live with over the years.

"Find Abe," were the last words he heard ringing in the cold air.

Contents

Chapter 1	1
Chapter 2	8
Chapter 3	15
Chapter 4	21
Chapter 5	31
Chapter 6	41
Chapter 7	48
Chapter 8	55
Chapter 9	63
Chapter 10	70
Chapter 11	81
Chapter 12	91
Chapter 13	98
Chapter 14	109
Chapter 15	117
Chapter 16	125
Chapter 17	134
Chapter 18	144
Chapter 19	153
Chapter 20	161
Chapter 21	172
Chapter 22	182
Chapter 23	192
Chapter 24	202

Chapter 25	214
Chapter 26	223
Chapter 27	230
Chapter 28	236
Chapter 29	245
Chapter 30	254
About the Author	*259*

Chapter 1

He was startled into waking by her mother's voice, soft but firm and clear. His eyes opened, and the voice rang all around him. He felt the fast thumping of his heart and remembered the colors around her mother's hands, felt as if they were enveloping him. Then he felt the warmth in his own hands, and he saw a red gel on his right palm, colors dancing around it, as they always did when he dreamed.

He closed his eyes once more, trying to remember the warmth of his mother's hands and willing the image from the dream to stay, imagining the colors flowing all around him the way they danced around his mother's fingers. However, even in his imagination, they slowly faded away, and soon he was only left with the darkness, the red gel on his right palm, and his hands grew cold. A familiar feeling of emptiness settled on his chest.

He opened his eyes and stared at the gray ceiling, feeling the warm softness of the red dream settling comfortably in his closed palm. It had been so long since he last dreamt, so long he thought he had lost the ability to do so, like everybody else.

He looked around the unfamiliar room, at the canvases all around him, some propped against the wall and others hung from them. At the far corner was his brother's work table, and it was littered with tubes of oil paint and used painting brushes.

He got up from the bed, the voice from the dream faintly echoing in his head. He opened the drawer on the bedside table that contained some empty bottles he saw the other night when he was looking through his brother's things. He took a small one, opened it, and poured the content of his palm inside the bottle. It was red. Not as dark as the wine-red blood in his dream, but more like the red of a ripe strawberry. He replaced the bottle cap and placed the bottle safely back inside the drawer, together with the rest of the empty bottles.

He was about to go out of the room when he caught sight of the bed, his brother's, with the sheets crumpled and the two pillows on the floor. Ever since he could remember, he would always move and roll around the bed in his sleep. His brother's constant admonishment to him rang in his head.

"Don't forget to make up your bed in the morning," he would say. "It's the very first space that is yours—you have to take care of it."

The thought created a knot in his chest, and he folded the blanket, smoothed the bedsheet, took the pillows from the floor, and arranged them on the bed. As he did so, the dream flashed before him again—the red bedsheets, his parents' dark figures forever etched in his mind, and his mother's words.

"Find Abe. Find him, and you will find the dream."

What did she mean? And is the disappearance of his brother connected to the missing dream in some way? Did he disappear to find the dream?

He felt the familiar pang of guilt that he had always felt since the day his parents were killed during a dream transfer.

Inhaling and exhaling a deep, shaky breath to fight off the feeling, he looked around the room. It was his brother's. Even when he still lived there, in their parents' house, before moving to a university dorm when he entered college, he did not get a lot of chances to be inside this room.

His brother was older than him by 5 years, and they could not be any more different. Abe was the smart one in the family, genius even. He always had his nose on his science books. If not exploring the mysteries of the cosmos, some new stars, or potential planets unknown to many, he would be marveling at some invention or device.

He remembered Abe being particularly interested in the science of dreams, that ever-elusive gift in their world. He had heard his parents talking about it in hushed voices, their voice sounding worried, when he was no older than 5 years old and they thought he could not understand them. From these hushed conversations he learned that ever since he was a child, Abe would dream sparingly, even less than most children. And as he grew up, the dreams stopped altogether. And it was normal, as with most kids, but Abe became even more obsessed with them when he lost the ability to dream.

Alec was born at a time when Abe was only starting to lose his dreaming ability. And when Alec was old enough to know what a dream was, Abe had lost the ability altogether. All that was left of Abe's dreams were the assortment of bottles lined on top of his dresser drawer, and he was obsessed with them.

In the beginning, their parents dismissed the obsession as the typical curiosity of a child, until they found Abe one day passed out from having discovered that it was possible to ingest the dream back and relive it, as adults often did. He was too young for it, and his innocent mind could not handle the dream. He almost died, and he spent several weeks in the hospital because of it.

Alec was too young at the time when this happened. He was two or three years old. However, although too young, there was a part of him that somewhat understood what was happening. It was that same part that told him dreams were special, but that they could be dangerous, too.

After the incident, their parents had to take away the bottles in Abe's dresser drawer, placing them under lock and key inside a glass cabinet in the master's bedroom. During this time, he noticed their mother, Abigail, spending a lot more time with his brother. Meanwhile, he spent more time with his father, Henry, in their garage. He fixed cars for a living, and he learned a thing or two about them from the time he spent watching his father work.

That was, until he noticed colors appearing on his fingers, dancing around them like they did around his mother's fingers. It was always a natural thing with his mother, so much so that he never thought to question it at that age. However, the same colors appearing around his fingers left him confused and curious. And that's when he abandoned his dad to his work in the garage and he started spending more time with his mom, trying to understand what was happening to him.

As they grew up, Abe's wild curiosity turned into a formal, disciplined, and scientific study of dreams, thanks to their mother's guidance. Henry and Abigail could finally breathe a sigh of relief, seeing their son find a productive way to handle his obsession.

As his brother got more immersed into dream study and as he slowly accepted the colors as a natural part of him, they retreated farther and farther away into their own worlds, and they never had a chance to be close to each other. While Abe spent more time burrowed in his books and studies, later apprenticing with a family friend who was a dream appraiser and worked in a dream shop, Alec spent more time with his parents and grew up like a normal kid, secured in the knowledge of his gift.

Looking around the room and feeling so far away from his brother, Alec's gaze landed on the work table on the other end of the room. He approached the table and found an A3-sized canvas lying there. On it was painted a bookcase filled with old books. The painting captured the dusty covers, some looking worn from use, the book case looking forlorn and forgotten. It was unfinished, with only the upper half of the painting done, to be completed.

He did not know whether his brother took up painting, or whether it was something he had always been interested in. He did not really know him. When Abe became old enough to pursue his interest in dreams, he moved to live with the old man he apprenticed for, a friend of their late grandfather, so he could learn more about dreams.

Abe only came home two months before he moved to the university for college, a time that the then teenage Alec spent with friends from school, often outside and coming home late. There was no time for them to reconnect even then. And then Abe was off to university, and life went on for Alec as usual.

Until that fateful day that still haunted him in his dreams, which changed everything and threw both his life and Abe's life into complete chaos.

He went out of the room and into the kitchen on the first floor to fix himself some breakfast. Going down, he had to pass through their parents' room, and he tried his best to suppress the knot that formed in his stomach when their last moment flashed in his mind...

Abigail holding both of his hands in hers, colors swirling around their entangled fingers. *Close your eyes,* she said. His mother pressed her thumbs on the pulse point in both of his wrists. And then his hands grew warmer and warmer, and a heaviness settled in his head as he saw colors swimming behind his eyes. And then his head grew warm and the colors got overwhelming.

He closed his eyes shut at the memory, and he hurried past his parents' bedroom down the stairs.

He had been home for three days, and during those three days all he did was sift through his brother's things, trying to find a clue about his whereabouts. He slept in Abe's room, telling himself it was in the hopes of getting into his brother's possible train of thought to help him understand his movements, maybe what was going on in his mind, during the last few days before he disappeared. In truth, there was a part of him who felt the need to be as close to his brother as much as he could—maybe that would tell him where he might be.

Chapter 2

After fixing himself some breakfast, he changed into his running outfit for his early morning run, a habit he had carried with him ever since he was a child, one he and his dad would do ever since he could remember.

Going out the door, he was greeted by the gray steel gate that secured every home in their neighborhood, each one looking almost exactly like the other—no fewer than three heavy locks in place to protect each home from robbery and home invasion that seemed to have become a regular, even accepted, incident in every community in their city. The keys jingled on his hands and a few colorful sparks flew off his fingers as he opened each lock and replaced it in the steel bars.

Once out, with the steel gate relocked in places, he could see nobody around, which was not surprising. This community was a ghost town, its residents almost always inside their homes. It was at least two blocks and several houses before he reached the community gate. He would often jog in the morning from their house to the main gate, and then he would jog back through another route within the community, passing by the back of their house and heading towards the other end of the gated community, which was another four blocks—their house was somewhat in the middle. Sometimes he would make one round, other time several rounds, depending on his mood and the weather.

Passing by the houses as he ran, it struck him how he never really knew the people living within those houses. The friends he had were all outside their community.

He passed by a smaller house with an open front porch, and he was almost surprised to see a young woman there. She was holding a mop, a pail of water a few steps from her, and she was looking down on the floor. Her movement created a monotonous rhythm as she slowly dragged the mop in one direction, and then the other, left, right, left, right, he could almost time it like clock hands ticking away in slow motion.

She probably heard the sound his feet made as he ran by because she looked up and stared at him. She was beautiful, the way her long hair flowed down her back and her eyelids slowly fluttered, but her eyes had nothing in them, like everybody else. They registered no emotion as they followed him while he ran past. He stared back, and he could see a big splotch of white on her right cheek, extending to a part of her upper lips. That did not subtract from her beauty, though, he thought. He raised his hands in a small wave, but the woman continued to just stare at her blankly while she followed him with her gaze.

He continued, and as he ran by each house, he would try to take a quick peek through the windows, catch a glimpse of the life of the individuals and families living inside those houses. Through one window, he caught sight of a woman facing a mirror, fussing with her hair as she tried to adjust her bangs to cover one part of her forehead and cheek. He slowed down, observing. There was a look of hurry and impatience in her movement as she peered at herself in the mirror, shook her head in dissatisfaction at what she saw, and kept adjusting her hair. Perhaps feeling someone looking at her, she turned to look towards the window, and they locked eyes. Feeling embarrassed at having been caught watching, Alec hurried on.

Reaching the community gate, he came across a tall and lanky guy covered in tattoos on his left arm, as well as in his neck. He was wearing a short-sleeved shirt, and black ink ran from underneath his sleeve, down to his arms and his wrist, stopping just before it reached his hand. The thin tendrils of ink creeping across his arm were both an art and a cover. There were tattoos on his neck, too, but even with the heavy inking, the splotches of white that had formed on the skin of his neck managed to escape through the un-inked part, creating a strong contrast against the black ink.

The man had his eyes fixed on the ground while he walked slowly. And as soon as he noticed Alec coming towards him, he absentmindedly brought his hand to his neck, as if instinctively covering it. He looked at

Alec with suspicion in his eyes but said nothing, and they went on opposite ways.

As he continued jogging, maneuvering to go back and head to the other end of the neighborhood, he ran his plans for the day in his head.

He had been home for three days, and he had found no clue. He figured the next best thing to do would be to check Abe's workplace, the dream shop where his brother had apprenticed and the same shop where he went back to work when he decided to come back home after their parents' death.

Abe was only in the university for a year before he went back home and decided to stay for good. After the death of their parents, without any discussion between the two of them, Abe stayed. He did not come back to the university. Instead, he transferred to a nearby school, not as prestigious as the first one but good enough, and he went back to work part time at the dream shop while going to school. When he finished school, he decided to work in the dream shop full time.

He didn't know whether his brother had friends, never knew any of them. As long as he could remember, Abe spent all his free time either reading about dreams and several other topics, or studying and working at the dream shop.

It made sense that it was the place for him to visit next. Perhaps there he would find a clue of his brother's whereabouts.

After his run, he went back home for a quick shower and breakfast and then headed out to the shop.

It was only several blocks away, and he decided to walk and reacquaint himself with the old neighborhood. They lived in a quiet part of the city, a gated community whose residents mostly kept to themselves.

Outside their gated neighborhood, it was another world. A few meters from the gate, the familiar smell hit him—an overpowering stench that seemed to have permeated the city. It's a general smell, an overall sense of decay, and more than just of any physical matter. The city itself seemed to have been in a state of decay for as long as he could remember.

Walking further, he was greeted by the noise of this outside world, and he braced himself for the crowd that he knew would be there in the next block. Here everything happened, and everything could be found—shops, a marketplace, restaurants.

Here, almost no one bothered to cover the splotches of white in their faces, arms, legs, and body. Everyone went about his business and simply accepted the white discoloration as a natural part of his physique.

The pale generations, they were called. He did not know the world that existed before this one; he was born into this, as were his parents. However, he had heard stories from them, passed on from their ancestors, of a world that was not dreamless and of people who were not pale and who didn't carry white splotches in their body.

Hearing the stories, to them it seemed like a perfect world. People were either white, black, or brown. They had either black, brown, red, or orange hair, either brunette or blond. They were pure.

Sure, they also heard stories about division between countries, about alliances and enemies, about greed and envy, about wars and death. But it was also a world of growth and transformation, a people with goals and plans and vision, a people of passion. And more importantly, they were people who could still dream.

Their grandparents could not exactly tell when the world changed—was it after a great war, a global epidemic, a nuclear accident? They could only tell of a time when people started to realize that they were dreaming less and less, until such time when they no longer could, and nights simply became endless darkness and non-existence. Only a few people were able to retain the ability to dream, and most of them were children. But even young boys and girls, they started to lose the ability to dream as they got older, save for a very few.

And even among those who could dream, their body seemed to have lost the ability to carry the dream. As soon as someone woke up from dreaming, the dream was expelled from the body, and one would find it in his hands—a small amount of gel-like substance that carried a specific color. And when people lost their ability to dream and dreams took on a physical form, they soon became the most valuable commodity in the market, rarer and priced so much higher than any metal or stone.

Chapter 3

"Move away!" He was startled by a booming voice from behind him, and he had just had enough time to move to the side before a bicycle carrying three boxes on top of each other came barreling down the sidewalk and hurtling past him as a man tried his best to keep a tight grip of the handlebar.

"You're stepping on my mat," a small whining voice blurted out, and he looked down to his left, by the side of the sidewalk, to find a small boy looking up at him. In front of the boy was an assortment of stuff, small trinkets, and random articles all laid out on a mat, and he stepped back when he saw he accidentally stepped on the edge of the mat.

"Ooops, sorry!" He squatted in front of the boy and peered at all the articles in front of him, taking a small metal wine glass with illegible carvings on one side. "This looks interesting," he commented.

"That's a 30-year-old metal glass," he volunteered. "Older than both you or me. You can look at the bottom of the base—the year it was made is carved there." He flipped the metal glass to look, and true enough the year written was 33 years ago.

"It was found buried in a blacksmith shop that burned down so many years ago, and the blacksmith was found buried together with it underneath all the rubble," the boy continued, reciting the story in a monotonous sound that indicated he had told the same story so many times before.

"It looks cool," Alec repeated. "Do you sell all of these?" He placed the metal glass back in its place on the mat and examined the other items laid there with curious eyes.

"Yes," the boy answered. "I help my mom sell these so we can buy food."

"How old are you?" He peered at the boy's face, trying to find any sign of white splotch but could not see any.

"Six," said the boy, extending a gloved hand. "I'm Karim."

He grinned at the boy's gesture, and then took the boy's hand and shook it. "Nice to meet you, Karim. I am Alec."

The moment their hands touched; the boy's eyes widened.

"Your… Your hands," the boy uttered, looking at his own gloved hand and at Alec's.

"Wait…" Alec was looking down at the colors dancing around his hands. "You can see them?"

The boy took his hand from Alec's and slowly removed the glove. At first there was nothing, and then he could see it—colors dancing around the boy's fingers, too.

"Your hands," Alec said in amazement. "They have colors, too."

"Yes!" the boy exclaimed, fascinated. "I have never met anyone with colored hands before!" His eyes took on new life, as if he was seeing Alec for the first time.

"I have met only a few," Alec said. "There are only a few of us here."

"I know," the boy added, a tinge of disappointment in his voice. "I sometimes hate them."

"Why?" Alec asked.

"Because I always must wear gloves. Mom is worried someone might see. She will not even let me play with other kids."

"The only people who will see are people like us," Alec explained. "Normal people can't see."

"I know," the boy nodded. "Even mom can't see the colors, but she said we can't take any risk."

"Where is your mother?"

"She's around here," Karim looked to his left, then to his right, searching. "She's selling bread and water. She goes to the stores to sell them to shopkeepers. No one really buys if we just stay in one corner. Maybe you should buy from her."

"I might." Alec laughed. "But I'm not really hungry."

"I have something people like," Karim's voice lowered to a whisper.

"Really?" He raised an eyebrow. "Show me."

"I can't," the boy's voice stayed low, and he looked around as if checking no one was within earshot aside from him. "My mom says I can't show it in public."

"What is it?" Alec lowered his voice in a conspiratorial whisper.

"My dreams," Karim's voice was almost inaudible, and he pursed his lips closed as soon as the word escaped them, as if he just uttered something he should not have said.

"Really?" Alec asked. In truth, outside of their family, apart from his own and the bottles of dreams his mom had, as well as the few bottles he had seen of Abe when they were younger, he hadn't really seen any other dream. He wondered whether they were like any of his own. "Do you have any right now?"

"No," the boy shook his head. "We keep them at home. My mom did not want to bring them outside, said it is not safe to show to people."

"Hmm, that's true," he agreed. "But you're selling them?"

The boy hesitated. "My mom said we shouldn't, that they have value more than money," he looked up at him in earnest. "But I want my mom to have some money so she doesn't have to always go away, so she can just stay home sometimes and rest. She is always gone; tells me she needs to find money."

Alec nodded, trying to show understanding, although oblivious to the truth that he could not quite capture the reality of the boy's situation—he had never experienced lack in his life. Their family never had to work so hard for money.

"Your mom is right," he told the boy. "Dreams are special."

"I know," the boy absentmindedly arranged the items on his mat. "But maybe I can sell them to good people. And you seem nice," he looked back up at him again. "You stopped and talked to me. Everyone else just walks by."

"Tell you what," Alec lightly ruffled the boy's hair. "Maybe next time we'll meet again, and you can show them to me. How many do you have?"

The boy raised his left hand, showing five fingers, and then on his right hand two fingers.

"Seven?" he asked, and the boy nodded. "Okay, that's good," he got up to go. "Maybe you can show them to me when I see you again."

The boy nodded again, and then he waved at him as he turned away. "Bye."

Children are lucky, he thought, imagining the collection of seven bottles the boy was keeping, perhaps in a small cabinet in their house, perhaps underneath his pillows. He imagined how he must be safely guarding the bottles, keeping it away from anyone's view.

And then his mind turned to the memory of the many bottles they had in the house—his and his mother's. Growing up, he didn't realize just how valuable the bottles were. He remembered feeling fascinated by the swirling colors, and every morning he would wake up with warm hands he would be excited to find a treasure in there.

It was like the legends of long ago that his mom would tell them about in her stories—tales of the Tooth Fairy, or the Easter Bunny, or Santa Claus riding a chariot pulled by reindeers and climbing down chimneys to leave gifts for nice children. He would wake up excited, and he would run to his parents to show the dream every morning, a swirling color inside the crystal bottle.

Chapter 4

His reminiscing was broken by the sound of beating drums and cymbals from a distance, the music getting closer and closer as he kept walking. He knew this community; some of his friends were from this part.

Turning another block as the noise grew stronger and closer, he found himself in a vibrant street filled with painted men and women, and they were in the middle of what looked like a festive gathering. People were gathered in a circle, and in the middle of the circle, right in the middle of the street, were old men and women dancing barefoot.

Like everyone else, their bodies were painted with vibrant colors. Their cheeks were rogue, a color matched by their lips. Their eyelashes glittered, and if one looked closely, many of them had green veins in their eyes, a sign of immense addiction to dream consumption. Their bodies were equally covered in paint, blue and red and yellow and pink. At first glance, it looked like they wore clothing of different color, but a closer look would reveal they had nothing for clothing—only naked skin underneath all the paint.

They found a way to cover the white splotches in their body with a burst of multiple colors on their skin.

Everyone's hair was long, including the men, and they sported different kinds of ornaments. The men's hair was either tied in red leather or braided down their back while the women's hung loosely, straight, and wavy, and had ornaments that ranged from small and shiny stone-like beads to dainty ribbons and colorful chopsticks arranged around like a crown on their head.

The old men and women who were dancing in the middle of the streets had loose and saggy skin that looked like they were part of the entire ensemble, complementing the colors and ornaments covering their bodies. They were dancing, lost in the music, green-veined eyes staring off and seeing nothing.

The rest of the colored men and women who were gathered around, encircling the dancing folks, were either beating on the drums that they carried, or banging the cymbals they held, or clapping their bare hands. There were children in the crowd, and they had less paint on their skin. They ran around among the dancing old men and women, their shouts lost in the noise and chaos created by all the drums and the cymbals and the clapping.

Walking self-consciously among the colored residents, he tried to keep himself as invisible as possible, but it could not be helped. His brown skin stood out among all the colors, and people looked as he passed by. A few hands reached out to touch him, but he managed to dodge them and quicken his pace.

At the end of the block, just as he was about to turn to the next corner, he accidentally bumped on a body, which quickly fell on the hard concrete with a thud.

"Holy hell!" a weak voice protested. It was a woman, her body covered in red and purple paint, her wavy hair almost covering her face.

"I'm sorry," he stooped down to help the woman get up, and she clutched his hand and brought it to her nose, sniffing it.

"You're pure," she said, not looking at him. She continued to sniff at his hand, and he quickly grabbed it back. "Hey!" the girl looked up, annoyance on her face, but it quickly dissipated in a look of disinterest as she stared blankly somewhere in the distance. The whites of her eyes were almost covered in green.

He debated with himself whether to help the woman get up, but she seemed like she was no longer there. Her body was right there, sitting on the black concrete, but her mind had already wandered somewhere. In the end, he decided to leave her to her inner world.

A block ahead, he could see the big signage of the shop, Romulus, in simple block letters, with each letter having a different color. It had an unassuming façade—two glass doors held by brown wooden frames and a gold-plated round door knob on each door. He peered into the shop before coming in, and there seemed to be only a few customers inside at the time, browsing through the items and looking around.

He pushed open the right door, and a twinkling sound rang inside the store. He was welcomed by the smell of lavender, and he could see where the smell came from. Lined on the counter were several candles lit and burning, the exact color of lavender, too.

A middle-aged woman in a yellow hat with fancy pink feathers and wearing thick spectacles turned to look at him, her gaze traveling from his head to his toe, and back, as she examined him, and then pursed her lips and went back to the shiny scarves she was rifling through in a rack.

On the far end of the store, a young man and woman who looked like they were his age, or close, were leisurely looking around, browsing through a vinyl collection, and showing each other new titles. They disappeared behind an oak cabinet with a label "Old Magazines" on top, although he could hear the woman softly laughing and the man saying something that he could not clearly hear.

He looked around the store and found that it seemed to contain so many different things, an assortment of items with no order in them. In one corner, there was what looked like a skeleton of a plant, lifeless twigs protruding and pointing everywhere, and they held in them several trinkets and accessories—gems and stones hanging from golden necklaces, shiny and multi-colored glass bangles, and rings of various styles and designs, so many of them they weighed down the dead plant. Beside it was a wooden cabinet carrying some curious machinery in it. There was a box-like machine with lettered tabs arranged in rows, like tiny stairs with letters on its steps. He pressed on one letter, and this lifted a steel rod, which moved forward towards a blank paper held in place against a metal tube. The steel rod retracted, and it left a letter on the page corresponding to the letter of the tab that he pressed. *Interesting*, he thought. Above the small machinery was written the word "Typewriter."

He was looking through other interesting artifacts when he noticed the young man and woman emerge from behind the wooden cabinet, the woman carrying some magazine, which she placed back on the cabinet before the two headed for the door. He got a better look as they walked away, and he was surprised to find that they seemed to have no white splotches on their faces.

He started walking towards them, hoping to catch them outside, when a door from the back of the counter opened and an old man came out hobbling. He slowly walked to the counter, and he noticed he had a cane helping him walk upright. He glanced towards the door and saw the young man and woman was gone.

"Excuse me," it was the woman in a yellow hat. She was heading to the counter, and Alec was blocking the way—it was crowded in the shop with all the items in there.

"Oh, I'm sorry," he moved to the side to allow her to pass and then followed her, wanting to talk to the old man.

"Hello, Bertha," the old man greeted the lady. He glanced at Alec, his eyes lingering on him for a bit before briefly moving to his hands, and then he turned back his attention to the woman without saying anything else.

He glanced at his hands where the old man looked, seeing a few light colors dancing around them, and then he instinctively brought his hands together behind his back.

Noticing what he did, the old man smiled while he turned his attention to the woman. "What do we have here?"

The woman carefully placed all the items she picked out on the counter, and it formed a small mountain in there.

"Please wrap each one carefully," she instructed, carefully arranging the items she had on the counter. "The last time, one of the ladies got broken."

"Yes, the old man answered," punching in the prize of each item on his computer, a small smile playing on his lips. "And you told me you dropped the bag on your way home. No wonder one got broken."

Bertha murmured something, and then continued to arrange her purchases on the counter.

They were a variety of personal articles and knick-knacks—a couple of silk scarves, a hair brush, metal pin accessories, and several ceramic paperweights depicting a woman in varying poses.

Once everything had been punched and the total purchase computed, Bertha handed a few bills to the old man. And while he was carefully wrapping each item in brown paper, the woman turned back to look at Alec again, peering at his face, searching him. "How old are you?" she asked.

"Uh... I'm... I'm 17," he answered, stuttering. There was a look of intensity in the woman that unsettled him.

"Hmm..." she continued to search his face. "You're clean. I bet you still dream." He wasn't sure, but he thought he detected a hint of suspicion, or anger, in her voice.

He stared back, not saying a word.

"Well?" the woman raised an eyebrow. "Do you?"

"Some... Sometimes," he answered.

"All wrapped and ready," the old man declared in a firm voice that carried authority.

The woman turned back towards the counter, took the handle of the cloth bag, and then weighed the bag on her hand before completely taking it. Leaving, she looked at Alec one more time, and then headed towards the door, continuing to murmur something he could not understand.

Alec followed her with his gaze until she finally went out the door and disappeared.

"She's a harmless lady," he heard the old man speak from behind the counter. "She asks a lot of questions, but she's not a bad person. Just bored, more like."

"She looks scary," Alec answered, turning to the old man and giving a nervous laugh. "You're Romulus?"

The old man nodded, and then asked, "You were curious about the young couple who were here earlier?"

"What?" he was confused.

"The young couple," the man repeated, smiling. "The woman with a heartwarming laugh."

"Oh yeah," he remembered, and then he gave the old man a closer look. "You know everything, don't you?"

"I'm an old man, after all," he laughed, and then continued. "They are both lucky, I guess, those two. They have small specks of white in their arms, noticeable but not too obvious. Perhaps it was their young spirit or... Perhaps it simply was their genes." He shrugged.

"I was trying to find them, and I couldn't find any. "But how do you know so much about them?"

The old man himself had white ears that extended to his all-white hair. Apart from that, his face looked clean.

"They come here almost every week," the old man explained. "And when you're an old man with all the time in the world, you will learn to notice everything."

He nodded, thinking. "I rarely meet people with no whites on their skin."

"They exist," the old man said, and then he gave him a once over. "Just like you."

He felt a sudden sheepishness. He was used to being stared at, but every now and then he would still feel the need to disappear when his being "clean" and different was pointed out.

He pursed his lips, not knowing what to say.

"So, you're here looking for Abe," the man said in a matter-of-fact tone. "But he's not here."

"What?" he was startled by his straightforward statement. "How do you know I'm looking for him?"

"Well," he peered at him again, searching his face. "You're his brother, Alec. He told me about you so many times."

"What?"

The man's smile disappeared, and he turned serious.

"I know about you," he started. "Abe told me about you. And did anyone tell you that you and your brother have a certain resemblance, from a certain angle?"

"Uh... no," he answered, unsure. "Do you know where he went?"

The man shook his head.

"He stayed here a lot when he was working here, when he was studying with me. He had made this his home for the past several years," the old man explained. "But about a year ago, he told me he needs to stop working in the shop, that there was something he needed to do. And then he came here less and less afterwards—once a week, then once a month."

"What did he need to do?" he asked, deep in thought.

The man shook his head again. "I don't know. He never told me. But about three months ago, he started coming here more and more again; his visits became more frequent."

"Did he tell you why?"

Another shake of the head. "No. Your brother is very private, and he doesn't talk a lot," and then the old man looked at him. "Except about you."

Me?

Why would his brother talk about him? They were never close.

Chapter 5

"What did he tell you?" he asked Romulus, who stooped down to get something from the cabinet in front of him and then emerged with two mugs that he placed on the counter between them. He stooped another time and then brought out a tray with a small thermos and a glass container filled with tea bags.

"He told me about your gift, said that you were special," he opened the glass container and took a couple of teabags, placing a bag in each mug. "He mentioned about…" his voice trailed off as his gaze travelled to Alec's hands, blue colors dancing around the fingers.

"You can see them!" Alec closed his fists, but he could not quite hide the colors—they only moved to cover his hands.

The man nodded, opening the thermos, and pouring hot water on the two cups. "I can."

"Do you have them, too?" he looked at the old man's hands as he replaced the cap on the thermos and placed it back on the tray.

He then laid out his hands on the counter, his fingers stretched out, and Alec gasped at what he saw—the tips of his fingers were all black.

"You…"

The old man stared at his hands and blackened fingers, and then closed his fists. "Yes…" he looked thoughtful. "The foolishness of the ambitious."

"I've heard of people like you," Alec continued, his initial shock slowly replaced by wonder and curiosity. "But I have never met one."

The old man smiled. "Well, now you have. Drink," he took the steaming mug while he moved the other mug towards him.

Alec took the mug and slowly brought it to his lips, blowing on the hot tea before taking a slow sip. It was peppermint.

"How…" he started to ask as he placed the mug back on the counter, but he could not complete the question. He realized he didn't know how to ask the old man the real question he wanted to ask. "I… I have a lot of questions."

The man chuckled as he continued to sip on his tea. "And I have a lot of time. I must tell you; I knew you the first time you came in, more because of the colors around your hand than any resemblance you have of your brother."

Alec looked at his own hands, colors dancing around then. And then he stared at the old man's face. "You are… Almost clean," he said. "Are you… Before this?" he gestured at Romulus' hands and his blackened fingers, and he was surprised at the light feeling of relief he felt at the possibility of them being similar.

The man smiled, the look of thoughtfulness still on his face. "Yes," he said. "I used to be just like you, but I've lost the ability to dream after this," he raised his hands.

"But my brother…" he trailed off. "Did he try dream conjuring?"

"Oh no," the old man vigorously shook his head. "I was already like this when I met him, so by then I knew the dangers of black dream spells. And that was one of my hard rules—no use of black spells to conjure dreams. Besides," Romulus continued. "Your brother was obsessed with dreams, yes. But all the things your parents taught you two, especially your mom, that was so deeply ingrained in him. He would never consider getting into dream sorcery."

"How did you get into it?" he asked, looking at the man's hands. They were burnt black, and all the fingernails appeared to have fallen off.

"Most of it was curiosity," the old man took another sip from his mug with his dead fingers. That's when he noticed that the pinky finger and the ring finger on his left hand were different from the rest—they weren't completely black; they were healing. "This store was passed on to me by my father, after it was passed on to him by my grandfather—it came from a long line of men in our family. It appears that my grandfather, and our ancestors before him... They were into black magic. They conjured dreams and sold them, profited from them, right in this very store."

Romulus looked around the store, an expression of fondness reflected on his face.

"It stopped with my father," he continued, a look of sadness crossing his face. "He tried his best that it stopped with him altogether, but I was stubborn and proud and curious," he sighed. "I wanted to continue what our ancestors started, thought it was something that made us special. And then this..." his voice trailed off, and he shook his head, smiling sadly. "It was foolish, and now I lost it. It has been so many years since I last dreamt."

"But your left hand... The fingers are not completely burnt."

"Ah, this," he held up his left hand and showed him the healthy fingers. "A product of hard work."

He then reached for a framed photograph on the cabinet by the counter and showed it to him. It was a photo of the old man, a little younger than he was today, and a bald man wearing a brown tunic. They were standing in an open field, and in the background was a mountain.

"Is that a monk?" he asked, peering at the photograph.

"Yes," the old man answered, nodding. "I met the man some years ago, and he showed me a way to cleanse myself. I went away for several months, up the mountains, to live with them. I learned how to purify my body, my mind, how to heal myself and slowly wash away the dirt and the death… It's a slow process, but I have these two healing fingers to show for it. It is working."

Before Alec could ask some more questions, the door of the shop opened and a man and a woman came in. They were both in black outfit, the man in an all-black shirt, denim pants, and boots while the woman was in a black jacket with a white shirt underneath and the same black denim pants and boots as the man.

At a quick glance, Alec could see both had a bit of white splotches on their faces, but they were not as much as everybody. The woman had a small white splotch above her right eyebrow while the man had a small one on the right side of his neck. Under the bright fluorescent light in the shop, he could also see both had what looked like small tattoos on the side of their face, above the jawline and near the ear—3 small dots arranged to form a triangle. The top dot was smaller than the two bottom dots forming the triangle.

They were heading straight to the counter, and he noticed the old man tense up at their arrival.

"I know you have questions for me about your brother," he turned to Alec. "Here," he took a key from a hook in the cabinet and gave it to him.

"Go upstairs. Ever since I fell and developed this limp, it had been impossible for me to climb upstairs, and I have entrusted that space to your brother. All his things are there; you might find something. Come find me at the back once you're done. Now go."

He took the key and headed towards the stairs on the left side a few steps from the counter, looking back to see the man and the woman talking to the old man before he finally climbed up.

He opened the door to a dark room, and he fumbled for the light switch on the wall. The room was, as he'd expected, spic and span, everything in proper order, the way Abe was in any space he was in. He was the same way in their home, and in his room mostly. Everything was in its proper place.

It wasn't a big room. There was a bed propped against the wall on the far end, a table placed beside it with some books and small bottles, some empty and a few swirling with colors inside them. They must be his brother's. He looked around, checking out a few paintings hanging on one wall. One painting depicted the shop's façade, with the name in bold letters and the door with the wooden frame. Another painting captured her mom's cabinet at home, the glass cabinet with its bottles of liquid dreams in different colors.

Apart from the paintings, one other thing that seemed to dominate the room were wooden book cases, several of them filled with books. There were books about physics, astronomy, geography, philosophy, all sorts of fields of study. There was also a section in the shelves dedicated to dreams and what they meant, how to appraise their value, or where they came from. He took a book from the shelf and flipped through the pages. It was entitled Dreams and Their Colors. He took it and continued with his search, not sure what he was looking for.

So, this was his brother's other life, where he spent most of his days when he was not home. This was all he knew about his brother, and not even well. His obsession with dreams. His intellect and his deep interest in learning. The way he tried to be a good brother to him all the years after their parents died, and the way their relationship had always been—all the good intentions there, but not quite yet. All his life, he felt that he and his brother were always skirting around each other.

That first year after their parents died, when Abe decided to come back home, Alec spent as far away from home and as far away from his brother as possible. He would hop from one friend's house to another, sleep over, and come home only to get clothing. Other times he would sleep in school, or in the garage where his dad worked and where he applied as part-time assistant to car mechanics who had known his father a long time.

Abe, on the other hand, turned back to his old obsession and spent most of his time outside of school in the dream shop. He learned everything he could about dreams.

That was, until everything came to a heed and they both had to face the things they were trying to escape and avoid for a long time.

Soon after Alec started working in the garage, he discovered drag racing and soon became a regular in the illegal race held weekly in the far side of the city. He was not very good at it, but it didn't matter to him. Racing helped him feel alive.

Sometime after his parents died, the colors in his fingers disappeared, and he thought it was because of his mother's death. Perhaps they were simply an extension of hers, and with her gone they were gone, too.

However, soon after he started racing, he found the colors would appear on his fingers while he was tightly gripping the steering wheel, heart racing, mind narrowly focused on the road ahead, the world quickly passing by and with only him and the car existing as one entity. During these moments, the colors in his fingers would come alive, pulsing with the fast beating of his heart, and he would get lost in them, transfixed. It was one of these moments when he lost control and, trying to swerve away from the other car he was racing with, he crashed against a dump truck parked next to a construction site.

He was lucky to be alive and to get out of the accident with only a broken arm and a broken rib from the hard impact against the airbag, coupled with several bruises across his body. The accident did not cause any serious damage, but it brought him face to face with his brother.

"This has gone on long enough," Abe said, facing him in the hospital bed. "I know I have not been the best older brother," his jaw clenched and unclenched. "But I hope we can make things better."

Alec stared down at his hands, cold and white. His left arm was in a cast. "I'm sorry," it was almost a whisper.

"I know," Abe answered. "And I'm sorry, too. I promised Mom and Dad I will take care of you, but I know I have been absent since they..." his voice faltered, and he breathed a sigh. "Let me take care of you from now on."

Things had changed since then. Abe made sure to spend more time home, tried to be a second parent to him. He made him promise he would try his best, too, and he did. They started with one rule—Abe made him promise no more sleepovers at his friends, that he would come home every day and they would have dinner together, at least that one meal. That created a new rhythm in their relationship.

He did not grow as close to Abe as he was with his parents, but they learned to be a family in their own way. Abe tried his best, that much Alec could say. Even though it was not easy for him to follow his rules, and there were so many times he broke them and defied him, his older brother had been patient with him.

They had had a good relationship until it was time for Alec to go to the university and move away thousands of miles from him a year ago. And he had to admit that he never really got to know his brother. He wasn't aware he loved painting. He never bothered to find out more about what it was he did, never once saw him at work all those many years he spent studying and working with dreams. They coexisted and lived in the same roof, but they lived different lives for the most part.

And now Abe was gone.

Chapter 6

He approached the bed inside that small room above Romulus' shop, looked inside the drawer in the bedside table but found nothing there except empty bottles, a notebook, and several pens. He leafed through the pages of the notebook but only saw random notes, computations and formulas that did not make sense to him. He took it and looked some more into the cabinets and drawers but found nothing else that could tell him where his brother was.

After some more searching and rifling through his brother's things, he went out of the room, closed, and locked the door, and went down the stairs, just in time to see the man and the woman in black going out of the shop.

He looked around but could not find the old man, and then he remembered he told him to find him at the back of the shop once he's done.

He went to the side of the counter and crossed to the door behind it, from which he saw the old man emerge the first time.

"Hello?" he called, knocking on the door.

"Come in," said a faint voice from the other side.

He turned the knob and pushed the door open. It was an entirely different room from what was on the other side. This room was so much dimmer. And where the shop contained random articles and items, this one contained all sorts of machines, things he had never seen before in his life.

One part of the ceiling was made of glass, and he could see the open sky. On one end of the room was a platform, and on it was a giant telescope pointing at the open ceiling—an amazing wonder to behold. On another end of the room was a small clock tower, at the bottom of which is what looked like a shallow cauldron with spindly steel rods pointing towards it, like those he once saw in surgical rooms. Against one wall was a shelf filled with bottles containing dreams, a mix of colors emanating a certain glow that gave the dimness of the room a mystical look.

"In here," came a voice from a small open door in one corner of the room.

He approached the door and came into a smaller room, as dim as the other room but with an open lamp on the table. He found the old man examining a glass slide under a microscope. On the slide was a green substance, and he added a colorless tincture to it, and it moved and changed in colors, transforming from one color to another before moving back to its original color, green. The old man noted the time it took for the complete transformation cycle to happen and jotted down something on a notepad.

"Did you find something?" he asked Alec, looking up from the microscope to glance at him before turning his attention back to the slide he was examining.

"I don't know," he answered. "I found a notebook, but I'm still not sure what's here. It's all gibberish to me, what I've read so far. And there was not much clues upstairs—it is all books."

"Ah," the old man chuckled, his forehead wrinkled as he added a drop of another tincture on the slide and nothing happened to the dream substance that was on it. "Your brother was always reading, always trying to absorb new knowledge. Did you find anything useful from among his books?"

"Just this," he showed him the book he took.

"Oh, that," the old man smiled. "I'm sure you're quite familiar with all of those colors."

"Not as much as I want to be," he flipped through the pages of the book. "It was Abe who was obsessed with dreams."

"Hmm, normal for anyone in want of something they don't have. I understand you never had to sell a dream before," the man raised his eyebrows at him, a smile playing on his lips. "You are privileged to never have the need for that. The people who come here, I've seen all kinds of them. Those who are so greedy and desperate that they live for selling dreams, and there are those who are always reluctant to part with their dreams but are simply out of options."

"I guess I am privileged not to have that need," Alec agreed. "Our parents made sure of that. And I have met very few people who are like me. We are an extinct species."

"I'm not sure I'm still part of that species. I lost the ability when I got deep into the practice of dream conjuration, almost died from it," he looked up from the microscope. "You never want to make that mistake."

"You already had the gift, like you said," Alec commented. "Why would you still need to conjure dreams? It can't be for the money. I mean, if there was something good with everything your ancestors did getting into black magic, it is all these," he gestured at the entire room. "You have everything you need."

The old man chuckled. "Ego, pride? I was young, and stupid," he looked back down into the microscope, peering at the non-changing green substance. "The limits we place on ourselves make a fool of all of us. We are told we are given a gift, and we do not believe it. Or if we do, we feel we need to earn it, to prove that we are worthy. And in that desire to prove something, we fall."

Romulus looked up from the microscope, and then asked, "Do you see this?"

Alec looked closer, and he could see the green substance moving. "Yeah. All I know about green dreams is that they fetch a healthy sum."

"Yes, yes, of course," the old man agreed. "But there is more to dreams than money. "We are called The Pale Generations because when we lost the ability to dream, we also slowly lost the color of our skin—we are slowly being drained of life itself. And yet all the world will tell you about it is the value of dreams in terms of money. No wonder there seems to be no way back."

He was taken aback by the passion in the man's voice, he was almost talking to himself.

"Do you see this?" the man asked again. "If you look closely, you will see the substance moving in a steady rhythm—it has its own heartbeat."

Romulus slid the microscope towards him, and he peered through the lens. Upon a closer look, he could see the green substance vibrating steadily. He almost found himself breathing with its movement.

"The darker the color of a dream, the faster its heartbeat," the old man said. "The content of darker dreams are deeper, more deeply rooted in the heart of the dreamer. The roots of some dreams are so deep they are planted not only in a person, but in the people who came before him. Some can be traced back to their ancestors. That is why they are so valuable."

The scene flashed back on his mind—the bloody bed with his parents lying on them, his mom touching his right wrist and pressing on his pulse point, his hand growing so warm he felt like it was burning, a dark purple dream that was there but wasn't, and him getting into his mom's consciousness.

"I am passing this on to you," Abigail's voice was tender but firm. "It is now yours, and you will carry with it the blood, the stories, the life of the people who came before you. It was passed on to me, and I am now passing it on to you."

And then a loud crash, a commotion somewhere far away, and then all darkness. Through the veil of semi-consciousness, some of the voices reached him.

"No!" it was his dad's voice. "Abigail!"

His eyes were slightly open, and some light filtered through. He saw two men beating up his dad while his mom was shouting in the background. And then both men took out knives, and it was all dark once again. The next moment of consciousness, he saw one of the two men approach him, and he tried his hand open. The dream, not having been completely transferred, now took on its solid purple form.

"The purple dream," he said, looking up at the old man. "Is that why Abe became even more obsessed with dreams after our parents died? Was he trying to find it?"

Romulus frowned. "Your brother has always had interest in dreams, and I think your parents' death and the dream being stolen only fueled his passion for it, gave him new purpose."

"Could it be the reason he disappeared?" Alec was surprised to hear a tinge of worry in his voice.

The old man could not give him any answer, and he left the shop with as much clarity as when he came, with his brother's notebook and the book on dreams in his hand.

Chapter 7

"Gibberish, gibberish," he murmured, growing frustrated as he flipped through his brother's notebooks and all he could find were random writings, numbers, and words that did not mean anything to him. "Where did you go, Abe?"

He remembered his brother's last call to him at the university several weeks ago, one of the rare times he mentioned his gift directly to him.

"Do you still have those colors around your fingers?" Abe asked, and he remembered wondering why his brother would bring that up after so many years.

Everyone in the family knew about it, even though only he and his mother could see the colors. They made it a point not to talk so much about it around Abe. His mother said she did not want his older brother to feel left out, and so it was always kind of a secret between them.

"Yes, I still have them," he said. The colors would come and go, but except for that year after his parents died and the colors disappeared for a while, they were always there since then. They were especially vibrant whenever he dreamed. There were a few times he would wake up from a dream feeling a burning hot sensation in his hands, and he would be jolted awake and find the colors glowing brightly.

"I've always been envious of them," Abe said during that phone call. "And even though you don't talk about it, I know that you were always different. You can still dream, just like Mom could. I lost that some years ago."

He was not sure what to say to him; they never usually talked about these things, or their parents.

"I know how close you and Mom were," Abe continued. "Before… Before they died…" he slightly choked on his words, and Alec felt him struggle to continue, but he did. "Mom told me to protect you, no matter what happens, to help you deal with… Everything."

"I didn't…" He started, and stopped before continuing. "I don't know why it was me, and not you. I do not know why I can do what I can and not everybody else." He found the words spilling out of his mouth in a rush of emotions. "I know I don't deserve this, and they would probably still be here if…"

"No," Abe cut him off. "Mom did what she knew she must, and I know you're doing what you can. Let me do what I can, too."

He remembered feeling an overflowing gratitude for his brother after that call, but he didn't really understand that Abe meant anything else about what he said.

Let me do what I can, too. What could he mean by that?

He was about to close the notebook when something caught him in one of the pages. It was three dots formed in a triangle, all equal in size, and beside it was the words "The League of the Dream Hunters."

He had seen those three dots, tattooed on the side of the face of the man and the woman in black who came into the shop, except the size of the dots weren't equal—the two bottom dots were bigger than the top dot. And the name… "The League of the Dream Hunters." He had seen that name somewhere, too, but where?

It's been a week since he came back, and he hadn't really been around. He stayed home looking for clues, went to the shop a couple more times, and during those times he learned more not only about his brother but about Romulus, too, and about the science of dreams, both the light and the dark sides of it.

He looked around the room until his gaze landed on his brother's work table.

"The painting!" he exclaimed, rushing to look at it. It was half finished, and it showed a bookshelf. Right there, on the left end, a book with the title "The League of the Dream Hunters." There is only one possible place the book could be.

Rushing to the shop, he found Romulus busy among his customers. He gave him a small wave and rushed upstairs to his brother's room. He searched through the bookcases, among his brother's many books on various topics and interests, and he found it right there, in the book case facing his brother's bed.

He took the book and sat on the bed, spending the whole afternoon reading the book and scanning through the pages. By the time he went down, hours had passed and Romulus was alone at the counter, with only one remaining customer looking through a selection of glass vases with gems in them.

"Spent a whole day upstairs, eh?" Romulus eyed the book he was holding, and he placed it on the counter.

"Do you know anything about The League of the Dream Hunters?" he started.

"Why are you asking about them?" the old man eyed him suspiciously.

He took out Abe's notebook and opened it on the page with the illustration. "I found this. And I saw it on the man and the woman who came into the shop the other day, the one who went to the back with you."

"Why are you asking about the league?" he noticed an edge on Romulus' voice. "What has that got to do with Abe?"

"I think he disappeared to join the league," he explained. "And you said so yourself—he had been leaving and disappearing for more and more time the past few months. He could be a league member already, for all we know."

The old man clenched his jaw. "That could be any random doodle. You know how your brother is, always getting into things."

"But look at this," he pointed at a writing at the bottom of the page, written by his brother in bold and block letters.

FOLLOW THE DREAM!

"What else could this mean but the dream stolen from our family, the one that got my parents killed?" his voice raised, panic starting to rise in his chest.

Romulus was silent for a minute, and then he exhaled, a defeated look reflected on his face.

"I told him it was a bad idea," he confessed. "He'd been relentless in his search for information. I once told him the league doesn't exist, that it was just a product of people's imagination, a projection of their hope for something to save them. But your brother is smart, and when he sets his mind on something he does not stop until he gets what he wants."

"So, it does exist, The League of the Dream Hunters?" he asked, more a statement than a question. "Is it possible he disappeared to join the league?" he asked. "And the man and the woman who were here the other day, they are from the league. Are you part of it?"

Romulus shook his head. "No. But my ancestors have always been connected to it; this store had always served the league, and they have been coming here for years to sell dreams, buy them, get dreams appraised, nothing too valuable. Your brother has met some of them a few times, worked with them on some of the dreams they brought here."

"Did he talk about joining? Showed any interest?"

"I told him it was a bad idea," the old man repeated. "The league has always been here for as long as I can remember, but the way they work in secret, the way they run their operations in the dark, it's hard to trust it. And especially not after all the transactions we have had and the secrets I have seen—not that I have seen much."

Abe spent several days reading more and more books about The League of the Dream Hunters, looking for more information. He scoured through his brother's books in the room above the shop to learn more. And by the time he was done with all the books about the league that he could find in his brother's room, he had formed the resolve to join and be a dream hunter and look for Abe.

Everything the books told him had given him an understanding of what the group was about, what it did and why, but it had also given him an even more sense of mystery—a sense of the group being real yet unreal, part truth and part fiction. However, he was holding on to Abe's notes in his notebook, some of which have started to make sense to him only when he learned more about the league. And he could not be mistaken about the three-dotted triangle he saw on the man and the woman at the shop. They were too specific to be coincidence.

In one of the pages of the book, he also found an address. Assuming that it was the headquarters of The League of the Dream Hunters or at least connected to them, he resolved to start there.

Chapter 8

It was a covered marketplace, so much like your average marketplace, crowded and noisy with its collection of stalls and vendors and buyers coming together in a chaotic rhythm. Except this one was under a roof and inside walls, with people coming and going.

He went in, and soon enough he was immersed in the flow of the people inside the marketplace. He navigated through the crowd trying to find any clue.

"Two for the price of one!" a lanky man with splotches of white covering his entire hands and most of his lower arms was holding two pigeons together.

"Free taste!" a lady was shouting over the noise. "I promise you it's juicy and sweet!" She was holding a plastic tray with slices of watermelon, offering it to passersby.

"Alec," he heard a familiar voice and saw Karim waving a gloved hand at him. He was carrying a tray that was hanging from his neck, and it contained all the items he was selling, some of which he had seen the first time he met him.

"Karim!" he approached the boy. "Do you sell here, too?"

"Yes!" the boy grinned, taking a quick peek at his hands—they had a faint trace of colors showing. "Are you here for anything?"

Alec nodded, and then looked around, not sure what he should be looking for and not knowing how to find it in the crowd. "Yes, I'm looking for two people… A man and a woman."

"Oh, I know!" Karim exclaimed. "Are you looking for him, too? The man who is like us?"

"What do you mean?" he asked the boy.

"The man," he explained. "I sometimes see him here, coming and going. He is like us. He has colors around his hands, too."

"Really?" Alec looked around, trying to see if he could find someone with colors in their hands. But there was none—all he could see were the people with white splotches on their faces and bodies. "Did you talk to him? Does he know you?"

"No," Karim was also looking around. "He doesn't know we are the same; he never saw my hands because I was always wearing gloves. I wanted to show him, but he looked scary and not very nice."

"There are only very few of us left," Alec turned his back on the boy. "I think we should help each other."

The boy nodded, thoughtful, and together they looked around the marketplace.

And then the boy, glancing at the far end of the market, suddenly pointed. "That's him!"

He followed the direction of Karim's finger and saw him: a tall, burly man in black shirt with his hands glowing blue and green. He was walking among the crowd, almost conspicuous if not for the colors in his hands. Trying to examine his face, that's when he saw it, exactly what he was looking for—a tattoo of three dots formed into a triangle on the side of his face, with the two bottom dots bigger than the top dot.

"I need to go," he told Karim, leaving. "I need to go after that man."

"I'm coming with you!" the boy followed him.

"Karim!" it was the voice of a lady, and they both turned to see an older woman carrying a tray like Karim's. Her eyes looked like his.

The boy turned back to him with a sad and solemn expression on his face. "I can't go with you, but will you tell the man about me? Tell him I saw him a few times and wanted to meet him!"

"I will," he smiled at the boy. "And I will be back to see you."

"Bye!" the boy waved his gloved hand at him, before he turned his back and walked towards his mother.

He followed the man with glowing hands as he walked among the crowd, through the marketplace, and until he reached a small entrance concealed by a black leather tarpaulin. The man parted the leather to reveal a doorway that led to a narrow alley, and he disappeared into it.

He quickly followed, fumbling through the dark side street, almost breathless as he felt the walls closing in on him. When he emerged on the other end, he came into what looked like a small courtyard with walls enclosing the area. There was nothing there except for a lone tree and what looked like a covered well beside it.

He went to the well and lifted the wooden cover, but it appeared too deep that he couldn't see the bottom. *He couldn't possibly have disappeared in there*, he thought.

Replacing the cover, he looked all around him. The walls were made from red bricks, all looking the same. He approached one side of the wall and walked alongside it, looking for any possible entrance, but couldn't find any.

Could he have climbed the wall to another side? He asked himself. The wall was at least 12 feet high, tall even for a 6'5" guy like him. And from the looks of it, the man was almost the same height as him. He continued searching, touching the wall's surface, and examining it trying to find anything unusual, until he came across what looked like a break in the wall's smooth surface. It looked like a solid stone door.

He pushed it, but it did not budge. There was no knob or handle, no indication of anything that could open it. He looked around trying to find clues, and the only thing he could find was the tree and the well.

He approached the well once more, examining the stone and bricks it was made of, the same as the wall's. Finding nothing, he removed the cover once more. Looking down and trying to see what was down there, he noticed a brick protruding from the wall around the well, standing out from the smooth surface of the round wall. Looking more closely, he saw the distinctive three-dotted triangle drawn on it. This must be the key.

He tried reaching down for the brick until he touched it, and he tried moving it but it did not move. He then pressed it back into what he assumed to be an empty space where the brick should be. It was heavy, but after sometime the brick caved, and he heard stone being moved. When he turned to look towards the sound, he saw the brick door had moved and was now protruding from the wall. He ran towards the door to examine it, and then with all his strength he moved the brick stone door to the side, revealing a dark entryway with stairs leading down.

It was too dark, and he had no light with him. For a moment, the question flashed across his mind—*What am I doing here?*

Then he remembered Abe. He remembered his parents, and how they died protecting a family dream he was entrusted with. *You cannot fail your family again*; he heard a small voice said. And whatever doubt he had was extinguished by that voice.

Grabbing the handrail, he slowly descended the stairs and into the darkness, slowly stepping down, one foot down after the other. At the bottom, when he stepped on the last step, it moved down and he almost fell, and he heard the brick stone door at the top closing.

He found himself in a dimly lit space, and on one end was a long tunnel. He followed the tunnel and walked in the dark for he could not tell how long, but it was long enough that he found himself asking a few times whether the tunnel would ever end.

He walked and walked, until he could finally hear a voice seemingly coming from the end of the tunnel. He walked faster, hoping to catch up with the man from the marketplace, until soon he could see light at the end. The voice grew louder and the light grew brighter.

"Aye, the supplies arrived last night," one voice said. "But I guessin' we need more, for the new recruits."

"The old equipment will do for now," another voice said. "Tell Norman to restock in time for new arrivals."

"Aye aye, Sir."

He heard footsteps going away, and he peeked in time to catch the back of a man leaving through another door. It was a wide hall, and the man from the marketplace had his back towards him.

And then sensing him, the man tensed and quickly pulled out a knife from his waistband as he turned towards where he was.

"Who's there?!"

He was hiding behind a pillar, and knowing he was found anyway, he stepped out behind the pillar and revealed himself, his arms up in a posture of surrender.

"Your hands!" the man exclaimed, looking at the colors in his hands as he also looked at the man's hand that was holding a knife, colors dancing around it. "Who are you? And why are you here? Did you follow me?" The man stepped towards him.

"Wait, wait!" he stepped back in fear. "I... I didn't mean to follow you. I saw your hands, from a distance," he tried his best to sound convincing.

"What's your name?" the man asked, looming before him. He realized he was so much taller than him.

"I'm Alec," he said, feeling smaller at the sight of this huge man. He had dark eyes, hair cropped so close to his head he was almost bald, and it made the tattoo on the side of his face so much more noticeable at a close distance.

They heard someone coming from the other door, and they both turned as two men arrived, both sporting a hairstyle like the man before him.

"Gregory," said one of the two men, eyeing him. "Finally! It is time you bring a recruit. Give Marlo and the others a run for their money. Is he any good?" the man nodded his head towards him.

The other man laughed. "Bet he's not a match to Jacob. Look at him, he looks scared as a duck."

The man called Gregory looked like he was caught off-guard, but he quickly recovered. "Guess you'll have to find out," he said with a grunt before throwing him a meaningful look and quickly scanning his hands, the colors now glowing more brightly.

"The Professor is looking for you," said the first of the two men. "And he doesn't seem like in a good mood," he added meaningfully.

The huge man grunted and then turned to Alec, adding in a rough voice. "Let's go!"

Chapter 9

Not knowing what else to do, he followed all three men towards the other door, which led to another narrow entryway and tunnel. After walking for what felt like half an hour, they emerged into a vast hall that looked like an old industrial plant, a chaotic space of people and machinery.

"Watch out!" a frisbee was rushing towards him, and after it was a girl running, looking panicked.

"Hey, watch it!" Gregory shouted.

He ducked just in time to avoid getting hit on the head, and Gregory was fast enough to catch the small girl before she barreled past and hit the wall behind them.

"I'm sorry," the girl looked like she was about to cry, looking at Gregory, and then at him, frowning.

Gregory took the frisbee, and with a grim expression said, "You're washing the dishes for lunch, and then you can have this back."

The girl's frown deepened, and then she hung her head low. "Okay."

She left to go back to her friends, her shoulders hunched in defeat. They were a group of young boys and girls, and they all whispered while looking at them before turning their back to find something else to do.

On one side of the room, there was a boxing ring, and a group of teenage boys and girls who looked around his age were surrounding it, watching a match between two guys. They were both topless, barefoot, both wearing a headgear, and engaged in a wrestling match.

Looking around, he noticed very little white splotches in the faces and bodies of the people around him. One teenage girl had a white line running across her forehead, a thin one, and that was it. It was not even noticeable, covered by her bangs, and he only noticed when he saw her wipe something off her forehead and the line was revealed. An older man passed by, nodding at Gregory with a look of what looked almost like reverence on his face, and he noticed a scar near his elbow, and it was covered in a splotch of white, as if it only grew there after the scar. The rest had small blotches of white, but nothing too noticeable.

On another end of the room, his eyes were caught by a girl and a boy, just a little younger than the group of children who were playing frisbee earlier. For a small second, he thought the boy looked like Karim, but upon closer look he found out he was a different boy.

He approached the two, mesmerized by the colors around their hands and what they were creating with these colors. He watched the young boy and girl as they made colored fireballs out of the colors dancing around their hands, bouncing them on the floor for several seconds and juggling them in their hands before they disappear into thin air. No one seemed to notice the colors, just him. Everyone else was going about their business.

"How do you do that?" he asked, and both children were so startled they dropped the colored balls from their hands. They were gone as soon as they hit the ground.

"Who are you?" asked the boy.

"You can see them?" the girl piped in.

"Yes," he showed them his own hands, colors dancing around them, and he saw their eyes lit up. "My name is Alec," he extended his colored hand.

"I knew it!" the girl exclaimed. "We're the same!" She extended her own-colored hand towards him. "I'm Chloey."

"Gregory!" the boy jumped up, his face brightening. "He's a Roy!"

He looked back to see Gregory standing behind them, his grim face loosening up a little.

"Roy?" he asked. "What's that?"

"That's just a name he invented for people like us," Chloey said. "He felt we should have a name."

"What, it's a good name," the boy grinned. "Can you guess what it means?"

He looked at the boy with wrinkled eyebrows.

"He's Peter," offered the girl. "We're siblings. I am older by a year."

"Siblings?" he asked, in both confusion and awe. Having someone like them in one family is very rare, and then to have two is nearly impossible.

"No guess?" Peter chimed in.

"Quit it, Peter," Chloey chided his brother. "You're so corny."

"Fiiine," Peter pretended to slump his shoulders. "You're no fun. What else could it be—it's rainbow! ROYGBIV, see? Because… Colors?" he threw his hands up in childish exasperation.

"Oh," he said with pretend awe. "That's interesting," and then he chuckled.

"Hmp!" Peter turned his back on him to go back to what he and Chloey were doing. "Stop lying."

"That's enough," interrupted Gregory. And then he gestured at Alec before turning around to walk away. "You, come with me."

"See you later," Chloey waved a small hand at him while Peter remained focused on creating his colored balls.

He ran after Gregory, who took a few flights up a series of metal stairs and went into what looked like a supplies room. Inside it were cabinets filled with uniform clothing like what everyone was wearing—black and gray shirts, leather jackets, as well as gears like wooden batons, chucks, and different kinds of dangerous-looking knives.

As soon as he entered, Gregory locked the door and turned to him with a snarl on his face. "You! Tell me who you are and why you're here!"

"I… I told you, I am Alec," he stuttered, trying to stick to the lie he said during their first conversation. "I saw you… And your hands… And I followed you here."

"Where did you come from? Tell me about your family," the man asked gruffly.

"My parents are dead," he answered.

"And…?" Gregory probed. "Don't keep me asking the questions, boy."

"I have a brother," and then quickly added. "He is away. Other than him, I have no other family."

The monster gave him a long, estimating look.

"Do you know what this place is?" he then asked. "Do you know what we do here?"

He debated with himself whether to tell the truth or to lie—what would give him the highest chances of staying?

He looked down, gathering the courage to say the words that would determine his fate here. And then finally, left with no other choice, he decided to say half-truth.

"Yes," he looked up, trying to look straight into Gregory's fearsome eyes. "The truth is—it's not only your hands that made me follow you. It is also that," he pointed at the tattoo on the side of Gregory's face. "I want to join The League of the Dream Hunters."

Gregory clenched his jaw. "So, you lied."

"I didn't lie," he answered, a hint of protest in his voice. "I also followed you for that, too," he gestured at Gregory's hands. "Ever since my parents died, I have lost my anchor… With them I was sure who I was, what made me," he felt a knot on his chest as the image of his bloodied parents on their bed crossed his memory. "My mom and I were the same."

Gregory was silent for a short moment, before asking another question. "And your brother? What would become of him if you joined?"

He shook his head, another half lie forming in his mind. "He's away, and we've always lived our own lives apart, ever since our parents died."

The man walked around him, sizing him up, or perhaps both him and his statements—the truth in them.

The knob on the door wiggled. Someone on the other side was trying to open it. Gregory strode towards the door and unlocked it, and a younger man entered, eyeing him as he did, and then Gregory. He was an inch or two shorter than Gregory, and so much younger. He had the same close-cropped haircut as the monster, wore the same black shirt underneath a gray vest, and sported the same tattoo as everyone else. The only difference with his tattoo was that the dots were of the same size, whereas those he'd seen so far were different—the bottom dots bigger than the upper dot.

The man's arm had a deep scar running from the back of his left hand and disappearing underneath the sleeve of his shirt. He gave him a quick once over, but he could not see any white splotch anywhere.

"Who's this?" the man asked, nodding towards him.

"A newbie," Gregory answered, not waiting for him to speak. "Fresh from outside."

The man nodded, sizing him up and down. "Let's hope he's up for it."

The man went to another side of the room and opened a cabinet, which revealed an assortment of weapons. He took a grenade and carefully placed it inside a pocket in his vest. He also took two swords and a small dagger before closing the cabinet door.

"We're headed to the Iclos," the man said to Gregory, and then turned to him. "Want to come with us?"

He looked back at the man, not knowing what to say.

The man turned to Gregory. "Is he ready?"

Gregory smirked, looked at him sideways, and then answered, "You'll have to see. Take him with you."

"Awesome! Okay, c'mon man," the man turned and headed towards the door.

He followed, not sure what he was doing.

"Stay alive, boy," he heard Gregory saying before the door closed behind them.

Chapter 10

They went down the flight of stairs and back into the hall they were in earlier. The man was walking so fast he had a hard time catching up.

"Alec!" Peter called from the other end of the hall. "Where are you going?"

He turned to the boy and shouted back. "I'll be back!"

The man crossed the hall and went back into the tunnel through which he and Gregory came in earlier. He ran after him.

The tunnel was dim, and Alec almost couldn't see where they were going. Before he knew it, they turned left where the tunnel forked, something he did not notice earlier when he first came through it. The two of them walked in silence, Alec catching his breath as he tried to also catch up with the man.

Before long, they reached what looked like a dead end, which he recognized as a brick door. Beside it was what looked like a keypad, and the man typed a series of numbers on it. The door moved from its place, and then the man pushed it open and slid it to the side.

He was momentarily blinded by the light, and when he opened his eyes, he found that they were outside. It was a forested area, with trees reaching almost as tall as the sky. Lined among the trees were two trucks, and about 25 men and women getting ready to board them. About half of them were older than him, the rest were about his age, with a few who were younger.

"Jared! Over here!" A guy that looked like he was just a little older than Alec called out to them, and the man approached him, with Alec following closely behind.

Jared handed one of the swords to the guy, who took it and waved it in the air, as if fighting an invisible enemy. Once satisfied with the feel of the sword in his hand, he placed it on a scabbard hanging from his waist.

"Who's this?" the guy eyed him with a friendly smile.

"New blood," Jared answered, taking a duffel bag from the truck to inspect its contents.

"New blood and you're taking him to Iclos?" the guy raised an eyebrow. "Are you crazy?"

Jared shrugged, closing the zipper of the bag, and placing it under one of the benches at the back of the truck. "Gregory saw no problem with it."

"Really? Gregory?" the guy examined his face. "You must be something good, then," and then he extended his hand. "My name's Carl."

He shook the guy's hand. "I'm Alec. Uh, I have no idea why I'm here. What's Iclos?"

Carl laughed out loud at what he said. "Oh man, you're in for something," and then he climbed up the truck. "Come on."

"Climbed in," he heard Jared behind him. "You're with us."

He clumsily climbed into the truck, and before long they were traveling in the middle of the forest. It was an open truck with two benches facing each other at the back, and there were about 12 of them. The road was bumpy, and he had to hold on tight to the metal railing frame above him to keep himself from falling.

"Guys, this is Alec," Carl shouted above the noise of the truck. "That's Emerson, Mikhail, Grace, Hannah, and King," he gestured at the men and women closest to them. "Alec is a new recruit."

He looked around the truck, and the first thing he noticed was how everyone was almost clean, with little to no streaks or splotches of white on their skin.

"New recruit?!" the girl named Hannah exclaimed. "What are you doing here?" She had black wavy hair that hung loosely on her back, framing her face in a disarray, and giving her a wild look. She could see no white splotch anywhere on her exposed skin.

He stared at her, not really knowing what to say. He was starting to feel like a fish out of water.

"And he can't talk, too," the guy called Emerson smirked. He was a broad-shouldered guy with muscles bulging from the sleeves of his tight black shirt. His hair was not cropped so close to his head like the others. In fact, it was longer than even Alec's own hair. Like the rest, he had the three-dotted tattoo, with all the dots in equal size. He had a malicious smirk as he looked at him. "I bet he pisses his pants the moment he encounters the first Maku out there. This guy looks scared as hell."

"I'm not scared," the words got out of his mouth before he could control himself. "I just rather keep my mouth shut when I don't need to open them."

"Ooh, now he talks," Emerson taunted him. "Bet you will be screaming later out there."

"Stop it, Emer," Grace interrupted. "Don't mind him. He is like that to everyone; thinks he is better than all of us."

"Oh, you bet I am," answered Emerson. "None of you has ever beaten me in the ring, remember? Not that no one tried," he turned back his attention to him. "Wanna try? I mean, if you survive today," and then he laughed out loud.

A gust of wind blew, and sand suddenly got on his eyes. Everyone took a black balaclava and head covering from their vest and put it on. He looked at one from the other, his eyes still stinging from the sand.

"We're close," announced Jared. "Be alert, everyone."

"You don't have head covering, too?" Emerson asked. "Why do you have to bring this guy, Jar, he looks clueless. He will get us all killed out there."

"Here, take this," Carl threw some cloth at him. "Wear that to protect your eyes."

Everyone stopped talking as they emerged from the forest into a vast dessert, the hot sun beating on the land and sand swirling in the air. The trucks slowed down as they navigated through the sand—it looked lifeless everywhere, and almost instantly he started sweating in the heat.

The trucks climbed a mountain of sand, and when they were on the other side, he saw structures in a distance.

"What's that?" he pointed at the direction of those structures.

"Target practice," Emerson was quick to answer, laughing, but he quieted when Jared threw him a sharp look.

Jared turned to him. "Do you know how to use a gun?"

"A gun?" he asked, unbelieving.

"How about a sword?"

"Uh... No, not really."

"Then you're left with this," he thrusted a dagger in his hand. "Let's hope you have a good throw, and that you move fast."

"What are we going to do out there?" he asked, eyeing their destination. The closer they got, the clearer it became to him what it was. It looked like a collection of concrete houses, stone squares clustered together in the middle of this hot and humid desert.

"There's only one thing you need to remember," Jared said, his voice hard behind the entire cover of his head, with only his eyes showing. "Do not get killed. Survive. If you must kill someone to do that, then do it. We will take care of everything else."

He stared at the dagger in his hands, noticing a feeling of terror growing at the pit of his stomach. No one said anything about killing. Perhaps he should have expected it, that killing was always going to be part of the job if he was to join the league, but not that early, and not without preparation.

It was quiet in the truck as they approached their destination. Even Emerson stopped talking. As they neared, he confirmed the structures to be stone houses, with open spaces for windows and doors, except now they were all closed.

"This place looks deserted," he stated what seemed obvious.

"They're hiding," Hannah said quietly. "They would have seen us coming from afar." She was holding a long knife in both hands, but she had a gun ready in a holster wrapped around her waist.

The trucks stopped, and everyone started to disembark.

"Eyes alert, everyone," Jared reminded, surveying the area. "Carl, take that side with Hannah, King, and Mikhail," he instructed, pointing towards the left. "You're with me," Jared turned to him. "Emerson, Grace, we'll take this side," he pointed in the opposite direction. "The rest, check that bigger barracks over there, see what you can find."

As the group from the other truck scattered around and their group went off in different directions, he followed Jared, Emerson, and Grace as they headed towards one of the stone houses.

"Emerson, Grace, at the back," he signaled with his hand for them to check the back while they went to the main entrance.

Jared placed his right ear against the wooden door, straining to hear any sound. Not hearing any, he slowly pushed the door open. The interior was almost empty, save for a wooden table in a corner.

"They're here," declared Jared quietly, examining what was on the table. There were three metal plates and leftover food, what looked like a half-finished meal.

There was an opening on one end of the room, a hanging tarpaulin clothing serving as the door. Jared slowly approached the entryway, a sword in his hands. He parted the tarpaulin and they found themselves inside another room, this one looking like it had been lived in.

On one end of the room was a makeshift bed on the floor, pillows and blankets all rumpled. On the other end was another door. There was a wooden cabinet and clothes hanging from a clothesline. The room had a pervading smell of stale sweat that was suffocating in the heat.

"They're here somewhere," whispered Jared, opening the cabinet to find some more clothes but nothing else remarkable.

And then they heard it—the sound of running footsteps coming from the other room. They quietly rushed towards the sound, and Jared slowly parted the tarpaulin clothing covering it.

"C'mon," he said. The room was bigger than the others, and it had heavy transparent plastic hanging everywhere, dividing it into sections. There were flies all around and the smell of decaying meat. The room looked like a slaughterhouse.

A human figure moved on the other end of the room.

"Maku," Jared whispered. "Hey!" he rushed towards the movement, his sword at the ready. Alec ran after him.

They found a man on the other end of the room, except it wasn't quite a normal man. He looked crazed, eyes wild, and a serpent-like tongue was hanging from his mouth. He was holding heavy rocks in both hands.

The man snarled, and then he threw both rocks at them before running away. Jared ran after him, Alec closely following behind, until they had him cornered on one end of the room.

The man looked at Jared, hissing like a snake, and then at him, eyes wild, and his mouth began foaming.

"Aaah!" he attacked, running towards him. Alec was caught off-guard, and he froze, almost hypnotized by the man's wild eyes.

"No!" he shouted, raising his hands to shield his face from the man's attack. Before the man could reach him, he stopped in his tracks—Jared rushed towards them and struck the man at the back, the blade piercing through his heart.

The man fell, his mouth still foaming and his tongue hanging from the side of his mouth.

He stared at the dead body wide-eyed, the dagger clutched tightly in his hand. "What is that?"

Jared looked down on the fallen man. "Maku. They are an anomaly created by excessive dream addiction or dream conjuring gone wrong."

"But his tongue," he added, looking down at the man's contorted face.

"Maku!" Emerson shouted from outside, and then the sound of gunfire followed.

They rushed outside through the back door, following the sound, and emerged to find Emerson and Grace engaged in a fight with several men who looked similar yet different from the other man inside the stone house.

"Die!" Emerson open-fired at two men who were rushing towards him. They did not have a serpent-like tongue like the other man, but both had two tentacles in place of each arm. Both men fell, but not before one of them wrapped one of his tentacles on Emerson's leg and pulled.

Emerson fell, losing grip of his gun. And the tentacle kept pulling at his leg even if the man on the other end had also fallen himself. He looked half-conscious, but the tentacle remained tight on Emerson's leg, slowly squeezing it, and pulling, as if it had a life of its own.

"Hey!" Emerson kicked at the tentacle with his other foot, but it kept its hold and kept pulling as it tightened. "Aaaah!" Emerson tried to reach for his gun, but it fell a little farther from him, out of his reach. "Die! Die!" he shouted as he kicked.

Jared rushed towards Emerson and, with a swift movement of his sword, cut the tentacle that caught Emerson's leg.

"Man, are you okay?" Jared asked, helping Emerson up.

Seemingly from out of nowhere, another man came from one of the stone houses and rushed towards Jared, a knife raised above his head. The man looked normal enough, with his crazy eyes and unkempt look.

"Watch out!" he shouted, and out of instinct he threw the dagger at the man. It caught him in the arm, but it kept moving, unfazed.

Jared was quick enough to evade the man's blow, and he maneuvered to try and take the knife from his hand. They both fell on the ground, wrestling with each other. The man got on top of Jared, and he caught the knife that fell on the ground. But just as he raised it, Emerson caught his arm and took the knife, stabbing him several times on the shoulder. Jared took the opportunity to get up and recover, finishing the man off with his sword.

Around them, several in the group were engaged in fights with the Makus.

"Where's Grace?" asked Jared.

"No!!!" they heard her shout from inside the stone house where they came from.

Chapter 11

They rushed towards Grace's shout. He took his dagger and followed the men inside.

They found several Makus where the room had previously been empty, and he found both Jared and Emerson facing off two Makus each.

"Stop it! Aaah!" Grace's shout came from the other room, and he rushed towards it.

He found her on the floor, shaking. A girl was beside her, holding her wrist, and Alec's eyes widened at the sight.

The small girl had colors in her hands, but they were red and black. She was holding Grace's wrist tightly, a sinister smile playing on her lips. She didn't seem to notice Alec in the room.

Grace was still shaking on the floor, and her lips were starting to turn blue.

"Stop it!" he rushed towards the girl, pushing her away. She let go of Grace's wrist, and Grace stopped shaking. He knelt to see if she is still breathing.

The girl looked sharply at him; her eyes had the same look as the others. And then she attacked, small hands extended. She closed her hands on Alec's neck, who was knelt beside Grace. He was caught off guard by a feeling of electric shock coming from the girl's hands, and the girl started to choke him.

He did not expect her to be so much stronger than she looked, and he felt her hands continue to grow hot and the skin on his neck started burning. And then he saw quick scenes flash on his head, and he was transported to another place, another time.

He looked at his hands, and it was the hands of a small child. He felt pain on his knees, and he realized he was kneeling on salt—the sharp grains were cutting on his skin. He heard himself crying, and a nearby mirror revealed him to be the small girl.

"I'm sorry, I'm sorry," he was saying in a girly voice, his hands extended. They were the same hands he saw, with red and black colors swirling around the fingers. "I did not mean to hurt my little brother."

And then he was much older, inside a laboratory.

"See that?" a woman's voice was saying. "Isn't it beautiful?" He marveled at the beauty of bubbles floating everywhere, red, and black in color, and when they popped, he watched in awe as memories floated by."

And then in the next flashback a commotion, and he was being taken away.

"Help me! Help me!" his shrill girly voice rang in the air, and then it all went black.

The scenes were cut short by the strong sensation of heat on his neck and the smell of burning skin, and he came to with the girl choking him. He could both see and feel the growing colors of red and black around her hands, and that brought him to action.

"No! Stop it!" he shouted, grabbing her hands, and trying to pry them away from his neck. When he met the girl's hands, he felt the heat on his own palms growing, and the colors around them also grew like flame surrounding his hands.

The girl appeared startled, and she yelped as she felt the intense heat, releasing her grip on his neck and drawing her hands away. He did not let go, holding the girl's wrists as she squirmed and shouted for him to let go.

"No, no! Let go! It's painful!" she cried, but he could not let go. He felt a rush of energy enter his body from the girl's hands through his, and another series of incomprehensible images flashed through his head. His breath stopped and he froze, unable to let go and oblivious to the girl's cries and shouts of pain.

The next thing he knew, he was lying on the floor and Jared was carrying the semi-conscious girl in his arms. Emerson was looking down at him, a curious look on his face.

"Wow, man, ruthless," he said, grinning. "You make little girls cry," and then he laughed out loud.

Alec got up and looked over at the girl, slowly gaining consciousness. The moment she saw him, her eyes registered fear as she looked at his hands, the intensity of the colors not subsiding yet. Jared let her down, and she hid behind him, trying to get away from him.

He looked around, and Grace was still slumped on the corner, rubbing her painful wrists. Her braided hair was a mess, and there were tear streaks on her face. He approached her, and she gave him a look he could not read.

He stooped down. "Are you okay?"

She nodded and tried to get up but fell back sitting.

"Careful," he helped her up to her feet until she was steady.

She looked at him in earnest. "I'm... I'm not sure what you did there, with the girl. And... I am not sure what happened, but thank you. You saved my life."

"I'm not really sure what happened, too," he answered. "But glad that you're okay."

"I want to know how everything happened," he did not notice Jared approach them. He looked around to see the girl being half escorted and half dragged by Emerson outside.

"What's going to happen to her?" he asked, a tinge of worry in his voice.

Jared looked at him curiously.

"You're really concerned about her? You almost killed the girl back there. It was a child, for God's sake."

"It wasn't his fault," Grace chimed in. "That's no ordinary girl. She almost killed me if Alec did not arrive in time."

"That's another thing," Jared said sharply. "I don't understand what happened here, but you better tell us. We need no secrets in this group."

Both Jared and Grace looked at him, expecting an explanation.

"I'm… I don't know what happened. That was a surprise to me, too."

"Why did Gregory recruit you?" asked Jared.

He looked down on the ground, at his shoes, and then confessed. "He didn't. I followed him from the marketplace."

"What?" Jared barked.

"I don't know if I should tell you but, I'm a…" he lifted his hands to show them, only to remember that they couldn't see the colors. "I'm a…" he tried to remember what the boy called them. "I'm a Roy."

"What?" it was Grace who asked this time.

"You mean…" it was Jared. "Like Gregory? And Peter? And Chloey?"

He nodded. "I think that has something to do with what happened to the girl, but it was the first time I experienced something like that."

Both Jared and Grace fell silent, weighing what they just heard.

"There you are!" Carl rushed in, followed by Hannah, King, and Mikhail. Emerson came in last.

"We loaded the girl in the truck," he announced. "She was so weak she could barely walk. I am not sure what you did to her," he looked at Alec. "But that seemed brutal, man. She was a little girl."

"She's not just a little girl," Grace interrupted. "I would be dead if Alec didn't save me."

Jared threw him another meaningful look before announcing, "Let's go!"

Everyone followed him.

"Don't mind Emerson," someone put an arm on his shoulder, and he turned to find Carl walking beside him. "I'm sure you did what you had to do to survive. Good job for surviving your first encounter with the Maku," he grinned at him.

Going out, he saw several more Makus lying on the ground, dead. He stopped on his tracks when he saw a man and a woman, both Makus he assumed, lying next to each other surrounded by pools of blood.

His parents flashed on his mind in those exact positions, in their bed, surrounded by pools of blood, and for a quick moment he thought the two were Abigail and Henry, mouth wide open in mid-shout and eyes slightly parted.

"Alec, c'mon!" Jared called.

He gave the two one last startled look, and then he followed the others back to the truck. The rest of the

Makus were being taken inside one of the stone houses, and there were shouting and commotion coming from inside.

"Shut up!" he heard King's voice coming from inside the stone house, and he was surprised to detect the anger that was behind the voice, so different

"What happens to the rest of the Makus?" he asked Carl when he caught up to him.

"The league works to rehabilitate them," he said, and then added. "… Those who can be rehabilitated."

"What does that mean? There is Makus that cannot be rehabilitated? What happens to them?"

Carl looked at him meaningfully, and then averted his gaze before answering. "We can't save everyone. Some of them are just too far gone."

"Are you saying they are killed?" he asked, disbelieving. Carl looked at him once more, but did not say anything. They walked silently back to the truck.

The Maku girl was already on the other truck, her hands tied to one of the beams. He caught her following him his movement with anger in her eyes.

In their own truck, there was another Maku boy just a little younger than him, trying to break free from the restraint that was keeping him tied to another beam.

"We're taking them back?" he asked Carl once they have boarded the truck.

"Yeah," Carl nodded. "The Professor needs them."

"The Professor?" he remembered the name mentioned by one of the first men he saw when he followed Gregory from the marketplace. "Who is he? And why does he need... Them?"

"They're Makus. They were once normal human beings, but addiction and greed turned them into something else," Carl explained. The truck started moving, and they headed on their way back to camp. "Some of them consumed too much artificial dreams that it twisted not only their minds but also their bodies. Others, the worse ones, those who ended up becoming something else, they were a product of malpractice in conjuring dreams—went too far and created dreams that consumed them."

"And then they started breeding," Hannah added, listening to their conversation the entire time. "They were so changed down to their DNA that they passed on the anomaly to their children."

He looked at the boy on the other end of the truck. He seemed normal enough, and then he remembered the girl back in the other truck. She seemed normal enough, too.

"That boy looks normal," he said. The boy had both a scared and a mad look, fearful and hateful in one, and he looked at them with spite in his eyes when he saw them staring.

"Maybe he is, maybe he isn't," commented Hannah. "That's why we're taking them. We do not only recover lost dreams in the league. We are also trying to find cure for the Makus."

"The Professor," he asked. "Is he the leader of the league?"

"You can say that, but in fact there's no one leader in the league," Carl answered. "We have several leaders taking care of different things. The Professor is just one of them."

"You'll meet them soon enough," it was Hannah. "How long since you joined the new recruits?"

"I… I just joined today," he answered.

"Today?!" Carl exclaimed. "So, when Jared said you were new blood, that was meant literally?"

"Most of the recruits, it takes month before they go out to join us in these missions," said Hannah. "And here you are!"

"Cool!" Carl raised his closed fist towards him, and he hesitantly raised his own to meet his in a fist bump.

"Guys!" Carl announced to the group. "It's Alec's first day as a recruit today!"

"First day?!" Emerson looked surprised. "No way!"

"Ask Jared," he said, turning to the guy who was sitting quietly on one end of the truck.

Jared just nodded.

"Wow, man, so you were in for a treat!" it was King, who grinned at him and handed him a chewing gum.

"Hmm, not bad for someone who made a girl cry," Emerson added, snickering.

"Welcome to the league, man," Mikhail tapped him on the shoulder several times.

As the truck crossed the dessert back to the forest, the chitchat continued, fueled by the remaining adrenaline and the relief at the mission finally being over and everyone being able to go home safe.

The truck entered the forest, and he felt, more than heard, a collective sigh of relief as they welcomed the security offered by the forest's shade. The chitchat died down, and everyone looked more relaxed, the adrenaline finally subsiding.

Chapter 12

They soon reached the concealed entrance to the barracks, and everyone got off the truck. That's when he saw a couple of injured men from their own, league members from the other truck. One had blood coming through a makeshift gauze wrapped around his thigh, while another one had his left arm hanging limply on his side, either broken or dislocated.

King took the boy from their truck, while another man took the girl from the other truck. The girl stared at him with a mix of fear and anger, looking at his face, and then at his hands that still had colors burning brightly in them. The color on the girl's own hands had subsided, although still visible to him.

"Take them to the Professor," instructed Jared. "He'd want to see them right away."

He followed everyone through the tunnel and back to the wide hall, and Gregory was waiting for them. He seemed surprised to see him, and his gazed fixed at his hands, the colors around them glowing more vividly than usual.

"You didn't tell me he just came in today, or that he was a Roy," Jared addressed the older man, a tinge of accusation in his voice. "He could have gotten us killed."

"Well, I see he's still here," Gregory answered, eyeing him. "Let me see that," he approached him and examined the side of his neck, and then he winced when he touched it. He did not realize his neck was burned, probably by the girl trying to choke him earlier. "That looks serious," said Gregory.

"Grace!" Jared called. "Will you take Alec to see Mirabella? Both of you need to be checked."

Grace approached them, still looking shaken. "Sure, c'mon." She beckoned at him to follow her.

"Are you okay?" he asked. He could tell she was walking a little unsteadily.

Grace nodded, still looking pale. "Just lightheaded, but I'll be fine."

She waited until they were out of anyone's earshot before talking again.

"I'm not sure how that happened, but it was from that girl's hands, right?" she asked, referring to the burn on his neck. "The same way her hands caused this." She showed her wrists to him, and they had burns, too. "Your hands probably caused the same for that girl, if not worse."

"I'm not sure how it happened," he touched his neck and winced at the pain. "I did not know my own hands could do that. It has never happened before." The colors had subsided, but his hands were still warm. "I just hope the girl is okay. I did not mean to hurt her."

Grace looked at him thoughtfully, sympathy in her eyes. "I know. And I am thankful you saved me."

They arrived in front of a small room, and from outside the door they could smell burning incense. They could also hear voices from inside. Grace knocked, and a soft female voice answered, calling them to come in. It was a small but tidy room, with a single bed, a table and two chairs, and a cabinet full of medicines and supplies. On one end of the room was an area separated from the main room by a heavy white curtain, and they could hear people behind it.

"That should work for now, but you need to rest. I will be back," they heard the same voice that called to them talking behind the curtain, and then the curtain parted and out came a petite woman with long flowing black hair that cascaded down her back. She was carrying a tray containing some medical paraphernalia.

"Grace, you're back!" she lit up when she saw the girl, and then slightly frowned. "Are you okay?" She looked from her to him.

Grace nodded. "Yeah, except for some burns on my hands and wrists. Alec here is hurt on the neck."

The lady placed the tray on the table and approached him, extending her hand. "Hello Alec, you must be new. My name is Bella."

He shook her hand. "Nice to meet you, Bella."

"Come sit down so I can look at your neck. You, too, Grace."

He sat down on one of the chairs and Bella took a closer look. "Was this burnt?" she asked. "It's swelling bad already. What caused this?"

Grace glanced at him without speaking, waiting for him to answer.

"Someone…" he answered, unsure how to explain it. He couldn't understand it himself.

"A Maku, you mean?" the older woman asked, and he was relieved she did not probe further. "I heard you brought back two young Makus. I hope the Scientist finds a cure for them, and for this entire… Condition."

"The Scientist?" he asked. "You have a Scientist here?"

Bella smiled. "How long have you been here? This must all be new to you. I think we have everything here, and in time you will meet everyone and find the right place for you."

Bella cleaned his wound, and he was told he was lucky it did not seem like a third-degree burn, although it could have been if he had been exposed longer to the heat.

Then she checked Grace, whose burns appeared more serious than him. It was obvious she was feeling some pain by the way she would clench her jaw while Bella was applying ointment to the burnt skin. He wondered how the small girl was doing; his hands probably caused the same thing to her.

"Gregory is looking for you, said you should see him after dinner." It was Carl. They were at the dining hall—him, King, Mikhail, Hanna, and Grace—when Carl arrived.

It was a cafeteria-style hall, and it was filled during the dinner hour. Men and women were seated together, and the noise of chitchat and laughter floated all around the room. He looked around, still in awe that most of the people here had little to no stains of white in their skin. The instances he saw some white streaks, they were small splotches and almost insignificant. Everyone had the same three-dotted triangle tattoo, which he learned earlier was the symbol for the league. All the members had it, and the leaders were distinguished by the size of the dots—they had the bigger dots on the lower part of the triangle.

He scanned the crowd, hoping he might catch a glimpse of his brother here. So far, everyone looked the same to him, and there was no Abe in sight.

All of those around his table were also wearing the same black shirt. He looked the odd one out in the group with the gray shirt he was given to wear. On one end of the room was a table with men and women who wore the same gray shirt as he was.

"That table over there," he looked over. "Those are new recruits like me?"

"Technically they're not recruiting yet," said King, chewing his food loudly. "They still must undergo a series of trainings and tests. If they pass, then they become recruits and new members."

"I think I should not be sitting there," he said. He could see some of them glancing his way and giving him a curious look, all while whispering among themselves. Some of the league members in black would also give him a look when they passed by their table.

"That's nonsense," Carl said. "We've been in a Maku mission together. You are one of us."

"You can't assume that," it was Hannah. "It will be up to Victor."

"Who is Victor?" he asked.

"He is the head of our group, the military group," answered Carl. "He handles all military matters, from missions like the one we had to strategic planning for recovering stolen dreams. Gregory is his right-hand man. He oversees training both old and new members.

"At the end of the trainings and series of tests, you need to be part of a group," said Hannah. "But you can't choose your group. A group leader must choose you."

"I'm sure you'll do fine," Carl said. "You have Gregory to back you up. You're his man, after all. He sent you on a mission on your first day. No one's done that before. And no noob has ever been on any mission on day one."

"That's if he passed the tests," he heard Emerson's voice behind him, and he turned to see him carrying his tray of food. King moved to give him space to sit, and he sat beside him. "And make no mistake, you won't be facing small girls here," he taunted.

"What kind of tests do I have to go through?" he asked, looking around the group. "And how dangerous is it?"

"Awww, you starting to get scared?" teased Emerson, a tone of mockery in his voice.

"C'mon, Emer, he's new," Carl chided the guy, sounding impatient.

"What, he can't take a joke, too? Fine, fine," he raised his hands in mock surrender. "You people are so sensitive."

"Where's Jared?" asked King, looking at Emerson.

"Meeting with Victor," he answered, and then turned his attention to Alec. "Gregory is looking for you, and he looks pissed."

"You better see him after dinner," Hannah suggested. "He's scary when he's mad."

The group laughed, but he could sense they were telling the truth.

Chapter 13

He looked for Gregory after dinner and found him in the training hall, doing some practice boxing just outside the ring.

"They said you're looking for me," he opened.

Gregory took a towel and wiped the sweat off his face.

"Do you know what it means to be wearing the shirt you're wearing?" he asked.

"I'm a recruit now?" he half answered and half asked, feeling nervous around this giant of a man.

"And it means the people you should be joining are similar recruits like you," he answered. "You can't hang around Jared's team until you go through the trainings and pass the tests."

"But it was you who asked me to join the group earlier," he protested.

"Consider that punishment for following me down here," he answered. "But you're in… If you pass the trainings. Starting tomorrow, you will join the new recruits. You will eat with them, sleep with them, train with them, breathe the same air they breathe. No special privileges, and they will be your only friends," this last statement, he uttered with emphasis.

He nodded. "I understand."

"And your… Ability," he added. "I got a report from Jared about what happened in the field earlier today. I'm not sure many here understand what happened. I am not sure you do, too, from the looks of it."

"It has never happened to me before," he confessed. "I'm not sure where it came from, or if the ability of the Maku girl triggered it."

"It is a gift, or it is a curse. And all I am saying is you should be careful," said Gregory. "Everyone here respects the unique gifts we have, and you are safe. But right now, no one knows if you, or that," he gestured at his hands. "Is going to be an asset to this group or a liability. We must make sure it is the former. But it will take a while, much training, and much discipline. And until then, I'm saying use whatever you have with caution—and control. Do not let it control you."

"I won't," he said, feeling an unexpected sense of security in the presence of the man.

Gregory gave him additional instructions and directions about the coming days and weeks as they go through the trainings, giving him some idea on what he could expect and what was expected of him. And to his understanding it all boiled down to one thing—learn to fight and survive. Everything else would come after.

The following morning, he woke up groggy after a restless night, haunted by the memories of the Maku girl. He felt like he had somehow absorbed some of the memories, and they had become a part of him. He would carry this feeling in the following days and weeks, and the girl would haunt him in his sleep.

As instructed by Gregory, he joined a few of the other new recruits to officially begin his training. They huddled inside a smaller room located right by the training hall. It was arranged like a classroom, with chairs lined neatly in rows and columns. Looking around, everyone in the group he was with shad a look of uncertainty in their eyes, like they were not quite sure why they were there. Some of them had small splotches of white in their skin, but nothing as bad as those he had seen outside the league. He wondered whether the first criterion for choosing members was their color.

A screen was placed in front, and a projector started playing—it was a recorded lecture providing information about the league and what it does.

"The League of the Dream Hunters is a group of elite individuals dedicated to solving dream-related crimes," the recording began.

He found out the league's work covered much more than just finding and taking back stolen dreams to return them to their rightful owners. The league also worked in curbing dream addictions, which had always been a widespread problem ever since he could remember. The green veins that appeared in addicts' eyes apparently caused not only the speedy deterioration of their mind but also the eventual loss of whatever it was that made them human, the fragments of their soul.

The league also took it upon itself to put a stop to the practice of conjuring dreams, which was a dark art that grew in practice a few generations after the dreams stopped coming. Self-proclaimed dream scholars claimed to have found a way to manufacture artificial dreams out of smaller amounts of dream gels. And while it showed initial promise, nature once again proved that any alteration to the natural state of things was bound to birth problems, even worse than dream addiction. The dreams that were conjured out of the experiments not only drove mad those who tried to consume them. Many were either seriously harmed or even killed. And those that did survive turned into something else—the Makus, creatures that were human, yet not quite. They were an unpredictable and uncontrollable race, and before long their population grew, with the natural Makus, those naturally born from Maku parents, showing certain powers, some of which the world had never seen.

He remembered Romulus and his blackened hands, a result of dream conjuring. The old man was lucky nothing more grave happened to him. And then the Maku girl—he couldn't quite decide whether she was guilty or innocent. Perhaps she was both.

The League of the Dream Hunters was led by several leaders, and each one had a curious name. The one they called the Professor oversaw all the league activities, and he seemed to be the leader of all the leaders.

The Warrior led the military activities of the league, and he knew this to be Victor, though he had never met the man. The Doctor was Bella, and she seemed to be the only female among the leaders, together with one of the two Gatheres, a pair in charge of keeping the league well supplied with all that the members needed to survive. The Weapons Master had a role like the Gatherers, except he dealt mainly with supplying all members and recruits with all they need for their military activities. And then there was the Scientist, the one in charge of all the research part of the league activities, specifically research on finding cure for the Makus and learning more about how they ended up the way they did, in the hopes of preventing more cases.

The league had been in existence for a very long time, but it had always been kept a private society. People had heard about it, but its status remained like those of old legends, with no one able to confirm the truth of its existence. It currently had a membership of a few hundred select members, and recruitment had always been personally done by members, never opened to the public. His entry into the league appeared to have been a rare accident—no wonder Gregory had always appeared too strict about the way he carried himself in the league. He was, officially, his recruit.

After the presentation was done, a small discussion followed where a league member entertained questions and he had a chance to meet some of the new recruits. This took a big part of their morning, after which they all proceeded to the training hall, which was already packed by then. He approached a group that was wearing all gray and who were having sword practice, each one paired with another, and everywhere he could hear the clang of swords.

He watched for a few minutes, until a guy in black, about a decade older than him, approached.

"Find your sword over there," he instructed, gesturing towards a corner where several swords were lying on the floor.

He looked over at all the metal and picked something, only to realize it was so much heavier than he could handle. He decided on a thin one with a pointy end, something lighter and easier on his hands.

"Here!" the same guy called him, and he approached. "Have you ever handled a sword before?"

"No," he shook his head. "Not really."

"Okay, try to block my attack," the man said, raising his sword and lightly slicing it forward.

In an instinctual move, he brought his sword forward to block the attack, only to find the force to be stronger and his sword flying off his hands.

"Oh!" he reacted in surprise, trying to get out of the path of the guy's sword.

"Okay, first mistake—your grip wasn't strong enough," stated the guy as he went to pick up his sword. "Hold it with both hands so you can place all your upper body force into, lean into it as you block or advance. Again."

The second time, he held the sword more firmly with both hands, and he was able to block the guy's attack, only for him to stumble backwards and fall.

"Proper footing," the guy taught him next, and for the next couple of hours he learned about properly gripping the sword, establishing firm footing, and the basics of attacking and defending. By the end of the two hours, his hands were shaking and he could feel his arm muscles tensed, sweat pouring down his back.

"Good start," said the guy. "Though you still have much to learn."

"Thank you," he said, grateful that it was over.

"I'm Chino, by the way" the guy replaced his sword on the scabbard around his waist. "I'm one of your trainers."

"I'm Alec," he answered.

"I'll see you around," Chino said. "Keep practicing."

"You were with league members yesterday," a guy older than him approached. "Have you been here a while? I have not seen you around."

"No, I haven't been here long," he answered.

The guy eyed him with a slight look of distrust. "Do you know anyone here?"

He shook his head. "Not really. I was with league members yesterday by accident. How long have you been here?"

"About a month now. We have been training a lot."

"You joined the Maku mission!" someone spoke behind him, and he turned to find a small guy—his age, but he was so much smaller, about 5'5" in height. "And they said you killed a Maku out there. How did you manage to do that?"

"It was by accident," he said, and he could not understand why he felt the need to defend himself. "And no, I didn't kill a Maku."

"Trainees are not allowed to join missions," the first guy said, and he was not sure but he thought he detected a hint of resentment in his voice. "Did you trick them?"

"Huh!" the small guy exclaimed. "How can you trick league members? They're among the most cunning people I've met!"

"I'm sure there's a reason you were there," the other guy accused. "And I'm not sure that's a good one."

The guy turned to leave, and the smaller guy followed, before turning back to gesture at Alec to follow. "C'mon, we'll introduce you to the others."

The other guy looked at him pointedly.

"What?" the small guy asked. "He's new, and he's with us. He will meet the others soon enough anyway."

The other guy looked back at him, unconvinced, but did not say anything.

The rest of the recruits were as alike as much as they were different from each other, seeming to come from all walks of life. He found the small guy's name to be

Wendell, and during the next few days he discovered he was an excellent archer. His aim was always precise, no matter the distance. Dexter, the other guy, was a good swordsman.

"Haaa!" he shouted, and the dagger flew from his hands, hitting the wooden target straight in the middle. Over the next few days, he realized he was getting good and comfortable with a dagger. He did not need to be close to the enemy to disarm him, which was the core reason for fighting that was taught in the league—never to kill or harm, unless truly needed. The goal was always to disarm.

Apart from the dagger, he'd learned how to handle a knife, which was crucial for close combat. As for the sword, although he had gained confidence in handling one, he didn't know if he was going to ever get better at it. The one thing he had been good at was his speed, and he could thank his running for it. He was swift and light-footed, and these had always worked to his advantage during the training.

Every time he was in the hall, he would always be on the lookout, hoping to find out whether his brother was there. He had always had no luck.

It made sense, he would tell himself. If Abe was here, it was almost impossible that he would be fighting. There was no violence in Abe's blood. He could be working for the Scientist—dream research was where he would be most useful. He needed to find the man and woman he first saw at Romulus' shop. They could be the members who recruited Abe.

"Listen up!" It was Chino. "You have been told about the series of tests you will have to pass before you have any chance of joining the league. And tomorrow, the first test starts. It will be one in a controlled environment, right here in the training hall. All the things you learned during the past few days will be put to the test, so be ready."

That night at the dinner hall, he could feel the restless and nervous energy around their table. Amid the usual noise of chitchat and teasing and laughter, there was some tension as everyone anticipated the next morning's test.

"Hey man, good luck tomorrow," someone tapped him on the shoulder. It was Carl, followed by King and Emerson.

"Give us a good show, yeah?" King was grinning, his teeth red from the red lollipop he had been eating. He turned to see Emerson with a malicious smile on his face.

"I'll be looking for you tomorrow," he said meaningfully. "Get ready for the ring."

"I can punch that guy's face in," Dexter said when the rest had left. "He always acts like he owns this place, treated the newbies like crap."

"Do you know what's going to happen tomorrow?" Wendell asked him.

He shook his head. "No, but I think I have an idea." He could picture Emerson's smile in his head.

Chapter 14

The next morning, they arrived at the hall early, to find that several rings had been added overnight—there were now four rings on four different ends of the training hall.

"This is it," Wendell said. "No turning back."

Everyone seemed to be there, and the recruits were all called to gather in the middle of the hall.

"Today is the first test out of three," Victor announced. He had a thick line of white splotch cutting across his face diagonally, running from his left forehead to his right jaw. But this did not make him look weak. Instead, it gave him a fierce, hard look, the look of a man who had endured battles. "You will step into the ring and fight in an unarmed combat—no weapons allowed. This is no longer training—this is a test of strength, speed, and strategy."

"Are we fighting each other?" Wendell whispered beside him.

And as if to answer that question, Victor continued. "You will be in the ring with league members. The one you will be fighting has specifically chosen you. Fight well."

A knot started forming on his stomach, and he looked around. He spotted Jared and the group, and he caught the eyes of Emerson, who was looking at him with a smirk on his face.

A league member called out names, and they proceeded to their assigned ring.

"Hannah, hey," he found her around his assigned ring. "Are you fighting today?"

"Hey," she looked unhappy. "Yeah, part of the job."

"I saw everyone," he said. "But where's Grace? I did not see her."

Hannah looked down, shaking her head.

"What happened?" he asked.

She looked back at him. "I am not supposed to tell you this, but I think you have a right to know, "she said. "Grace has been unwell since… Since that day at the desert. She is not doing okay."

"What? Where is she?"

Before Hannah could answer him, he heard his name being called in the ring.

"Alec!"

He stepped into the ring and looked around at all the faces looking up at him, league members and recruits alike, searching for the one face he was sure he would find.

"You have been chosen by Emerson."

He saw him step into the ring, that smirk still frozen on his face.

"Finally," he announced, taking off his shirt. "Remember when I said no one's ever fought and defeated me in the ring? That is true."

Emerson raised his fists, ready to fight, and he reluctantly raised his to defend against his attack. He did some boxing practice during the past few weeks, but it was never his strong suit. He was good at running, could be everyone in speed during the training. Perhaps he could use that in the fight.

Emerson advanced and threw a punch, but he was quick enough to duck and avoid it, which he successfully did for the next few punches thrown by his opponent.

"Good speed, newbie," Emerson taunted him. "But you can't escape me forever."

"Hurry it up," reminded their referee. "Quit beating around the bush. Show us some offense."

He stepped forward and attempted a punch aimed at Emerson's face, but the latter was quick enough to avoid his fist. The next moment, Emerson's fist encountered the side of his body, and he felt the air on his lungs left him at the force of the blow. He clutched at his stomach, and Emerson used the opportunity to deliver another blow to the side of his face, one that brought him face down on the floor. Everything was dark for a split second, and he tasted blood in his mouth.

"Get up," he heard Emerson's voice from the other end of the ring. "Is that all you have?"

He shook his head, clearing his vision, and got up, resuming his position.

"Lesson number 1," the man had both fists raised, ready. "Always be on your guard."

Emerson advanced and threw a fist forward to hit his face, but he evaded the blow and simultaneously threw his fist towards the other man's body. He felt his fist connect with Emerson's ribs and heard the other guy's grunt when it did, and he hugged him close as he kept punching him on the side, delivering blow after blow.

Emerson managed to get out of his grasp, and before he knew it the guy had him pinned on the floor, straddled on both sides by his legs, and Emerson had free access to his face. The guy just kept punching, delivering blow after blow. He managed to shield his face with his hands, and in a desperate attempt to get out from under him he threw a jab at his throat.

This caught Emerson off-guard, and he used the chance to get out from being pinned. He threw down his body on him from behind, trying to bring the man down. However, the guy was too big and too strong for him, and it did not take long before he was back on the floor face down and the guy had him pinned down.

"Thought you could take me down that easily," he whispered, a note of menace in his voice. "You thought wrong."

He felt the air leaving him, and he couldn't breathe.

Outside the ring, he caught a glimpse of Gregory, looking at him with an unreadable expression on his face.

"Concede!" he heard Hannah saying, and as he started to slip away and lose consciousness, he remembered what Hannah said earlier about Grace, that she was in bad condition… And then there was a quick flash of the memory of the Maku girl, the same glimpses into her head like the first time—and in a quick moment his surroundings changed, and he found himself shouting while he was being taken away. He was once again in the

"I will kill all of you!" she shouted in between sobs, before the crying stopped and only her clear voice echoed as she shouted. "You will all die!"

He remembered it, and then Grace, before everything turned dark as he started losing air.

He woke up back in the barracks, alone. It was afternoon. He could feel some pain on his sides, where he got some beating, but overall, he felt okay. He went straight to the training hall, where the test was still ongoing. He found Dexter nursing a bloody left cheek.

"Alec," the guy greeted him, holding an ice pack against his swollen face. "You, okay?"

He nodded. "Yeah. How's it going here?"

"Nothing unexpected," he said. "Most of us took a beating, although Wendell is apparently so much stronger than he let on. He gave one of the league members a good fight."

He looked around to see Wendell talking to Victor from across the hall. He had a bandage wrapped around his right hand. And then around the other ring, there were Carl and Hannah talking to each other.

"See you around," he patted Dexter on the shoulder and went to the other ring.

"Oh man," Carl said when he saw him. "You got us worried for a while there. No one's ever beaten Emerson in the ring, at least not among us. You never had a chance with him. That guy was a boxer even before he came here."

Hannah shook her head while clicking her tongue. "He only had himself to blame," she said to Carl, although looking at Alec. "There's nothing wrong with conceding. It would not be taken against you," she chastised him. "At least not at this point."

"Emerson's had it for me since day one," he said. "It was only a matter of time."

"You are wrong right there, newbie," Emerson declared, taking a seat right beside him. "I did not single you out, not in the way you think. But I do love a great challenge. You have my respect for seeing it through to the end."

He caught Hannah roll her eyes. "Boys and their pride."

And then he remembered what she said. "What happened to Grace? You were telling me something about her before the fight. Is she okay?"

"You told him?!" it was Carl. "Gregory specifically instructed to keep this from him until after the tests."

"Gregory wanted to keep this from me?" he exclaimed.

"He deserved to know," Hannah answered Carl. "They were the ones together when it all happened."

"Where is Grace, and what exactly is her condition?" he asked.

Hannah looked down and slowly shook her head. "I'm not sure. We haven't seen her in a while. But the last time we did, she was looking bad."

"You said it started during that day with the Makus, but it's been a few weeks ago since then. Was she ill this whole time?"

"She never recovered," the girl heaved a sigh. "It was on and off for a while, and we thought she was just tired from all the trainings and the work. One day she'd feel a bit better, and then the next day she'd be sick, until..." her voice trailed off.

"It seems she was being poisoned from the wound she had on her hand," Carl added. "I heard about rumors of her hands needing to be amputated."

"They can't do that," Hannah protested. "How can she be part of the league without hands?"

"You don't think it's possible?" asked Emerson. "There is a lot of work here to be done. I am sure she will find a place here."

"Are you seriously considering that? That she is going to lose her hands?" the girl was clenching her jaw, torn between feeling anger, and trying to keep herself from crying.

"It's just a possibility," Carl came to Emerson's rescue. "You saw how she was the last time. Her hands were turning black."

"Where is she?" Alec asked. "Is she at the clinic?"

Hannah nodded.

Chapter 15

He went to the clinic to check what exactly happened with Grace, but he arrived just in time to see her being wheeled out of the room by two men, Bella following close by.

She was asleep and looking pale, and he noticed a patch of her hair has turned white, including the skin underneath them.

"Where are you taking her?" he asked in a strained voice.

Bella turned to look at him, a downcast expression on her face. "I cannot do anything to help her now," she said. "The Scientist will help find cure for her. Maybe she will have a chance with the new medicine they were trying to develop."

"The Scientist?" he asked. "New medicine? What is wrong with her?"

The woman shook her head. "I don't know. It's beyond my capability at this point. I have done everything I can to help her." And then she left to go after the woman, leaving Alec even more confused.

Then he remembered the one person who might have an answer for him, the one person who knew about the colors, the dreams. He went to find Gregory. He found him cleaning a gun in the training hall.

"What do you know about the Maku girl we took during the last time we raided the settlement?" he opened, sitting beside the man. "What did she do to Grace?"

Gregory placed the gun down on the table before turning to face him.

"You're a recruit," he answered, looking at him with all seriousness in his eyes. "You have no business getting your nose into league affairs—not yet. Who told you about Grace?"

He ignored his question.

"That girl, she's like us. I mean, she may be a Maku, and she used her skills in an entirely different manner," he explained, remembering the darkness he felt when the girl used the colors as her weapon, touched him, and burned his skin. "But there is a part of her that is like us," he continued. "Maybe she can save Grace, or maybe we can."

"Boy, you have not been here long. You have not seen half of it. I understand feeling the need to do something, but one thing you will come to realize when you become part of the league and discover what you are capable of," Gregory paused. "Is just how limited your abilities are—at least in the world the league is moving in. And to be part of the league, to be a dream hunter, you need to learn to let go of the things you cannot control. And to let the people who can do something about it handle the matter."

"But Grace looks dying. We're just sitting here, waiting? We won't even try to help?"

"Trust me, if our help is needed, we would know."

He sighed. "What's going to happen to Grace?"

"No one knows," Gregory admitted, shaking his head. "This is the first time we've had something like this. That girl, we have not encountered anything like her before."

"How is the Maku girl?" he asked. "She tried to use the colors on me," he touched the skin on his neck, which has not completely healed at this point. "But I fought her with the same thing—my colors. I did not even know it can be used as a weapon, to harm other. It just happened. Do you know how she is?"

"No," Gregory shook his head, taking the gun off the table and resuming with cleaning it. "She's upstairs with The Scientist."

"Who is The Scientist? And what is the league working for, exactly? I thought it is all about the recovery of stolen dreams," he asked. "But apparently there's so much more."

He heard Gregory heave a sigh, as if preparing for a long explanation.

"Yes, there is so much more, as you have probably learned by now. The lost dreams, they're a small part of the league's work. This curse we have, it covers more than just dreams. It has not only created a generation that is pale and incapable of dreaming, it has created a lot of other defects, too."

"The Makus," he said. "I've seem dream addicts outside, their eyes blank and their minds lost and empty. And I have seen people, with burned hands, from trying to conjure dreams," he remembered Romulus and his shop. "But the Makus... They are an entirely different race. How come they have survived this long and no one really knows about them, except the league?"

"Our generations, or at least most of us... We have lost a part of our humanity when we lost the ability to dream," Gregory explained. "And that part where humanity used to be, it has remained empty for most of the population. But the Makus, in that empty space that humanity vacated, something else took over—something dark."

"Isn't it that the Makus were a result of dream conjuring that went wrong?" he asked, remembering what he learned.

"That's true," Gregory agreed, inspecting the gun he was cleaning more closely. "Most of the first Makus were a result of dream conjuring gone wrong. But we found that most of them had an alteration in their genes that made them more susceptible to becoming something else."

"Does that mean those who became Maku were meant to become Maku right from the beginning?"

"Perhaps," Gregory answered. "Or perhaps the experimentation with dreams simply triggered whatever it was they had in their genes, causing them to transform into Makus. And now they are everywhere, and they wreak havoc more than dream robbers caused."

"The Maku girl, she has power so much stronger than we have," he remembered his encounter with the girl, and he looked at his own hands, a feeling of terror beginning to form at the pit of his stomach. "But… But I had the same effect on her. When I tried to pry her hands away from my neck, my hands burned her, too."

"Has that happened to you before?"

"No," he explained. "I swear it has never happened before. I have never hurt anyone. I did not even know how it all happened."

Gregory grew silent, thoughtful, slowly nodding his head.

"The girl, how is she?" Alec asked.

"She'll survive," answered Gregory. "She had burns in her hands. We assumed it was from her own, from her burning Grace's hands, and your neck. You said you caused it?"

He nodded. "I think. I felt my hands burning when I tried to take her hands off my neck, and she screamed in pain. I never intended that to happen."

"We haven't had any case like that before," Gregory said. "Not like the Maku girl, and not like you."

"So, am I like her?" he asked, unable to hide the worry in his voice. "The darkness, is it in me, too?"

Gregory shook his head, exhaling a sigh. "I don't know. But we have studied the Makus long enough, and I am sure they will soon learn about this new ability, whatever it is and wherever it comes from." And then Gregory added, "You should focus on your training for now, on the next two tests. You'll learn all about these soon enough—if you pass and get in."

The thought weighed on his head during the next few days of training. He always knew he wasn't normal, knew that he wasn't like most of the people around him. Growing up, his mom had always said he was special. But was there more to him than just that? Was there a darkness hidden in him that he did not know about?

"Hey guys," they were at the training hall, and he approached Carl and King who just finished a sparring practice.

"What's up, dude?" Carl wiped off the sweat from his forehead with his arms. "You ready for your next test?"

"I think so," he shrugged. The test was going to be in three days. "Do you know where they brought the Maku girl?"

"The girl who is the reason Grace is in a coma right now?" King's voice hardened. "They should have killed her. They should have killed every one of the Makus."

Carl was silent, and then he said. "They're trying to find a cure for the Makus. The younger they are, it seems the better the chances of curing them. But that girl, she's different from the rest of the Makus we encountered. I do not know what kind of cure they can do for her."

"A cure is not the answer," King continued. "Why do we waste our resources on them? They all need to be eliminated."

"We aren't much different. The Makus started out like us," said Carl. "We just went different paths."

"We all have choices," King reasoned. "The Makus made the wrong ones, and they brought down innocent people with them because of those choices. They need to suffer the consequences."

Carl shook his head, but did not say anything anymore. King left, still seething with anger.

"One of his closest buddies here was killed by a Maku," explained Carl. "And he's made it his mission to kill every last one of them."

He stared after King, who was leaving the hall.

"The Maku girl, do you know where they took her?" he asked Carl.

"I don't know, but upstairs, perhaps," he answered. "With the Scientist—he deals with the Makus, and he's been trying to understand how to cure them and bring them back."

"I've heard of this Scientist several times now, and the Professor. Have you met any of them?"

"No, not really," answered Carl. "I saw the Professor once, from afar, but I have never met him. And the Scientist, I've heard about everything he's done, but they never come down here. We only ever deal with Victor, and Gregory. Only very few of us get to go upstairs."

Chapter 16

The next chance he got, he found himself knocking on the door of the clinic to talk to Mirabella.

"What can I do for you?" There was no one at the clinic at the time, and he found the lady on her desk, scribbling notes on a pad. He sat down on the chair opposite her.

"How's Grace doing?" he started. "Is she getting better?"

The lady looked at her intently, and then answered. "I don't know, to be honest. All I can tell you is that she is in much better and much more skillful hands right now."

"Did you treat the Maku girl, too? The one they brought here that same day?"

"No, I don't deal with Makus. It is the Professor and the Scientist who work with them."

"Do you think they will allow me to see her, or Grace?"

Bella stopped writing and put down her pen. "Shouldn't you be more concerned about your own trainings and tests?"

"I just… I just want to see them, know how they are doing."

"Stop obsessing about these things," Bella's eyes had sympathy in them. "They're out of your control, or mine."

"I know, but…" He could not bring himself to admit the guilt he'd been feeling, about the possibility he might be one of them, that he might have deadly capabilities, too.

"Look," Bella said. "I know what you are, and I know you might still be trying to understand yourself and your capabilities. But this is not the time to rush into things. You're almost part of the league, and when you are, you can have the answers that you want. Do not jeopardize that."

She found Bella's advice reasonable, and she kept the advice in mind as he prepared for the next test. The next few days saw them learning how to handle guns, from gun assembly to shooting practice. And then the day came for the next test.

"In the first test, you fought in the ring," it was Victor. He asked all recruits to gather a day before the test to give instructions and make announcements. "This time, you will fight outside the ring, in the real world."

There were murmurs of mixed anticipation and anxiety among the group.

"You are going to face real enemies. We received intel on a factory being used by one of the biggest dream syndicates operating in the city. Tomorrow is going to be a raid of that factory. It will be led by Gregory, and you will be with actual league members to complete this mission."

The murmurs continued, and he could feel an energy of restlessness and excitement growing across the hall.

"We only have two goals," continued Victor. "One is to collect and take back all the dreams they have stolen, and then bring them back here so we can find the owners and return them. The second is to bring the perpetrators to justice. It is our priority to take them back here alive, especially their leaders. We need more information about their operation, how wide it is, and where else they keep the dreams they stole—we believe they have headquarters inside and outside the city. So, we need them alive, we need their information. But," Victor hardened his voice. "If it comes down to it and it's between your life and theirs, between the life of your fellows and their life, we will not hesitate to defend ourselves and to kill—but only if necessary. Is that clear?"

"Yes!" they answered back in unison.

"Everyone, get enough rest tonight and be ready at dawn tomorrow," barked Gregory. "Team leaders, stay behind."

Everyone dispersed, while Jared and the other leaders followed Gregory to another end of the hall as they discussed final plans for the following morning."

"Do you know where we are heading?" They assembled at dawn the next morning and rode several vans, weaving through what looked like familiar streets to him in the dark. They continued driving for a long time, until they seemed to have crossed the city and everything became strange to him.

"No idea," Wendell answered, peering through the dark window of the van they were in. They were carrying guns, and he had a small one with him that he had been practicing on the past few weeks. He also brought his trusty dagger; one he had learned to master over the course of his training.

Their van stopped, and the door opened to reveal Jared. "Our target is that building over there," he pointed to a lone building in a wide parking lot. "In about 15 minutes, a vehicle would arrive carrying a whole package of bottled dreams. The moment that happens, we are moving in. Get ready."

The van was parked in a side street, concealed by darkness from anyone who might pass by. He could not see the other vehicles, but he assumed they were under the cover of darkness, too. They went out of the vehicle one by one and moved to take their places near the building, with Gregory, Jared, and the other league members taking the lead. It was a large three-storey building, and it looked unoccupied. There was no light on inside, although there were two cars parked near the entrance.

The group surrounded the building, and it wasn't long before another car arrived, three passengers inside it.

The driver parked beside the two cars already there, and then looked around before getting out. He was followed by another man from the passenger seat, and a third one from the back. The latter was carrying a big briefcase, and the two men from the front flanked him on each side as they walked towards the building entrance.

Jared and several league members emerged from the shadows and signaled for them to move to the door. They followed quietly, their guns at the ready. They entered a hallway and emerged to see rows and rows of wooden crates stacked together. He saw the three heading towards the other side of the factory, and they quietly scattered around to surround the area.

The three stopped and waited around a rectangular table and placed the briefcase on top of it, and two men emerged from the shadows. One was a tall, lanky guy wearing a coat and a fedora while the other one was a stout man, shorter but bulkier, with authority emanating from his aura. He held a gun in one of his gloved hands.

"Everything went well on the way here?" asked the man with the hat.

"Yes," answered the man with the briefcase, opening it to show the contents. Bright colors—bottles and bottles of dreams were inside it. He took a bottle with a purple and yellow gel and held the bottle against the lamp. In the dim light around them, the bottle shone like a gem. "You will like this one. It will fetch no less than three million."

The stout man in gloves took the bottle and gave it a closer look, examining the contents, and in that moment, he saw the signal from Jared.

"Dream hunters!" shouted Jared. "Raise your hands and don't move!"

In a flash of movements, commotion ensued and he fired his gun outside of training for the very first time, aiming for the leg of the stout man who was running away with the single bottle of purple and yellow dream. The other man in a fedora hat ran in a different direction carrying the rest of the briefcase.

He missed his aim, and he ran after the man, Jared and other league members following close by. The man went behind one of the rows of crates and fired a few shots their way. In his frenzy, all shots also missed, and he stayed hidden behind the crates.

"We are members of the League of the Dream Hunters!" Jared shouted, gesturing at them to move closer to the man's location. "We have hunters all over your factory! There is no chance you can get out of here. Give back the bottle, and we might take you alive."

Everything was silent at the other end, and as they moved closer, he saw light emanating from behind the crates. He followed the light, signaling to other league members to move slowly towards the source.

Soon, they had a view of the man. He had taken off his gloves, and he could see colors around his hands—he was a Roy, too. The man opened the bottle and took the liquid gel on his palms.

"Stop!" he shouted, and they emerged from the shadows, all guns pointing at the man.

The man had a look of panic on his face, and before they could do anything he clasped the gel tight on his hands and firmly pressed on his wrist, right at the pulse point. He lost focus on his eyes, retreating to his inner world as the dream started getting absorbed.

"No!" he ran towards the man, but he was too late. By the time he pried the man's hands open, the gel is gone, already fully absorbed by his body.

Almost instantly, the man started writhing on the floor, issuing painful shouts.

"Aaaah!" he shouted, emitting a sound of anguished cry as he clasped his head in his hands. "No! No!"

Alec's eyes grew wide, and he tried to shake the man, tried to take his hand and press on his wrist, hoping to take the dream out of his body. However, the man was so strong. In his writhing, he pushed Alec away. Alec slid across the floor, hitting one of the crates.

He lost his breath from the impact, but he stood up and ran back the man, attempting to try again. Jared held him back.

"There's nothing you can do," he said, watching as the man writhed in pain, battling with the dream he had consumed, apparently too strong than his mind could handle. "It's too late."

He watched the man's face contort in pain, his body shaking, and saw the colors in his hands quickly change from red to green to blue, an assortment of colors until his hand turned darker. After what seemed like eternity, the shouting ceased, and the colors on the man's hands disappeared—his hands had turned black. He still clasped his head in his hands, curled in a fetal position whimpering, his eyes blank and unfocused.

Footsteps came running, and Gregory emerged.

"What happened?" he asked, his eyes quickly drawn towards the whimpering man. The man's once frightening demeanor had melted, and he was like a baby in his position, helpless. There was no color at all in him, except for the dream that was now clasped once again in his hands. The color had turned dark purple.

He knelt beside the man, who was still shaking and quietly whimpering. He found the small bottle container beside him, and he scooped the gel and placed it inside the bottle. He turned his gaze at Jared, demanding an explanation.

"He took the dream," Jared started. "He tried to consume it."

"Why would he do that?" Gregory asked, looking back at the man. Then he noticed his black hands. He turned to Alec.

"He's... He's a Roy, too," Alec said. "I saw his hands when he took off his gloves."

When Gregory turned back to the man, he found him lifeless. His head was still clasped in his hands, and he was still in a fetal position. His entire head and his hands had turned white by then.

Gregory placed an ear against the man's chest, checking for any heartbeat. Nothing. He shook his head and stood up. "He's gone. Round up everyone. We have everything we need. We better go back."

"But..." he had so many questions. He looked around and noticed that most of the members and recruits were gathered around them, and there were several curious looks pointed at him.

Outside the warehouse, they loaded several crates into two trucks. The syndicate members they captured, they loaded on another truck. Before the sun rose, they were on their way back.

"You're a Roy?" asked Wendell. His voice was merely above a whisper, but it sounded like it was ringing in his ears.

He nodded, still feeling shaken by what he had witnessed.

Chapter 17

"Bring those upstairs," Gregory instructed the men as they hauled the crates off the trucks. "Jared, take care of these crooks. Victor will deal with them." Gregory started walking away.

"Gregory!" he hurried beside the man. "How many times do these things happen? How often do people die because of dreams?"

"More than you can imagine," Gregory answered, not looking at him as they continued walking up a flight of stairs. "Dream addiction is only the surface of it. People's greed will stop at nothing, and the consequences have only become graver."

He followed Gregory to his quarters. "I thought I know everything there is to know about us, about this world. But the things I've witnessed so far…"

"Sit down," Gregory took a chair by a rectangular table and gestured for him to take the opposite chair. "What have you learned about your ability before you came into the league?"

"What?" he asked, baffled.

Gregory looked at him.

"I... I know that unlike most people, I can still dream at my age," he looked at his hands with vivid colors dancing around them, pulsing with his fast heartbeat from the adrenaline that had not subsided yet. "My... Ability, I got it from my mom. I have been exchanging dreams with her since I was a child. She was always preparing me for the dream transfer, to pass on the dream that was handed down to her by her own parents."

Gregory looked thoughtful, listening to him.

"But I never received the dream," he continued. "It was stolen during the dream transfer, and it caused the death of both of my parents," he paused, trying not to choke with emotion. "My mom always told me the dream transfer would reveal more of my gift, and it would help me understand what I'm capable of... But that never happened, and I stopped trying to know. I just wanted to forget all of it."

"I'm sorry, kid," Gregory gently shook his head. "This dream business has made chaos out of this world. But you're in the right place. You have a better chance at finding that lost dream here in the league."

Alec debated with himself whether to tell Gregory about the other reason he was here, looking for Abe. In the end, he decided to keep quiet, unsure whether he could fully trust the man.

"Now that you're here," continued Gregory. "Your focus must be on passing the last test. This one will be different. You are not going to be tested together, equally, in the ring or in battle. In the next test, we will discover who you really are and whether you have a place in the league."

"What does that mean?" he asked.

Gregory looked at him. "You said you haven't had a chance to understand who you really are, but you need to trust yourself. If you are to pass the last test, you need to be confident in who you are and what you're capable of. And you must trust the entire process."

"What is the test going to be?"

"I cannot tell you that," Gregory answered. "But I can tell you that it will have something to do with your ability. Since the day you came here, there have been eyes watching your every move, your every reaction to every situation, assessing your strengths and your weaknesses. Even if you've kept your ability hidden from most of your fellow recruits and league members, trust me that the right people know about it. And all the observations made during your training and your performance in the first two tests will be used to design the perfect test that will determine your fate here."

"My ability," he looked down at his hands, colors dancing around them. "The test will have something to do with... This." It wasn't a question as much as it was an acknowledgment of what he knew now would be about to happen. "What if I don't pass? What if they don't find me capable of using the ability that I have?"

"Trust the process," Gregory reiterated. "The test will reveal what needs to be revealed."

He went out of Gregory's room without receiving a satisfying answer to his question.

On the day of the test, they gathered at the training hall. There were no extra rings set up, nor were the weapons on display and ready to use. Instead, he saw several individuals in attendance that he had not seen before. It seemed like everyone was there. He looked around, still hoping to see the face that was the reason he was there.

He'd been with the league a few weeks, and during those weeks he was always searching for Abe, to no avail. The full schedule of the recruits and trainees left him very little time alone to do more searching. They were almost always confined to either the training hall, their quarters, the dining hall, or outside when they went on missions. And they were almost always together.

Looking around, he stared at the new faces he saw. The Gatherers, the couple responsible for procuring the needs of the league, turned out to be the man and the woman he first saw at Romulus' shop. They were responsible for handling most of the business the league had with the outside world.

Mirabella was there, too, together with a man named Norman, which they called the Weapons Master. A younger man, perhaps a few years older than him, was among the crowd. Unlike all the other leaders, his tattoo had all three dots of the same shape. He stood out not only because he was wearing a white coat amid all the blacks and grays in the hall but because Alec caught him looking straight at him, as if trying to read him. He also seemed unperturbed by all the commotion happening in the room, like he was inside his own bubble, unaffected by the noise and chaos around him. He heard someone refer to the man as the Apprentice—he was apparently working with the Scientist.

Mirabella stepped in front first and called out names. "Keith, Lionel, Zee, Anabel, with me." Those who were called stood up and followed the lady out of the hall.

The Weapons Master stepped in front next. "Walter, Brigo, Sophia, Johan, Eleanor, Mikhail, with me." The men and women called followed the man outside the hall.

The rollcall of names continued, threes and sevens and tens, and at one time up to 15 names were called at once to join Victor. When it was the turn of the guy in white to step in front, he looked straight at him.

"Alec, with me," and then he turned away towards the entrance of the hall. He hurried to follow the man.

"Just me?" he asked, falling in step beside the man as they continued walking.

"Yes," he answered, not looking at him. "For this batch, yes. But you will not be the only one taking the test today."

And just as he said that, Peter and Chloey appeared.

"Alec!" Peter exclaimed. "I knew it!"

"We're testing together!" Chloey held his hand and walked beside him. "Hello, Nicolas!" she cheerfully greeted the man in white, who turned to her with a small smile.

"This is your first time to go through this test?" he asked the twins.

Chloey answered. "Yes. We trained first before going through this."

"But we did not do the other tests, like you did," added Peter. "Because we're just children, we will do this test directly. We cannot fight yet."

"Of course," he nodded. They emerged in front of a steel door, different from all the stone doors in the place. This one had a keypad, and Nicolas pressed on a number combination. The door slid open, and in they went.

They came into a dim room that reminded him of the room in Romulus' shop, the backroom he occupied with all the machinery and the cabinets filled with bottles and bottles of dreams of different colors.

"Take your seat," Nicolas gestured towards a couch before disappearing behind another door.

"Do you know what kind of test we will go through?" he whispered to the two children.

"I hope they let me make the dreams dance!" Peter exclaimed excitedly.

"What do you mean?" he asked, his eyebrows furrowed.

"Do you want to see?"

The boy took out a white handkerchief and several bottles from his pocket. One bottle contained sand. The other bottles contained dreams, gel of different colors.

"Hmm," he looked at the different colored bottles thoughtfully, and then finally picked a bottle with blue gel inside it. "You'll like this one."

He laid the handkerchief flat on the table and poured the sand on it. Next, he poured the blue gel on the sand, and it didn't take long before it absorbed all the sand and the blue gel became brown blue. Peter then took the gel and sand in his right hand that was now glowing.

He lifted his left hand, and his glowing fingers moved and hovered over the blue brown gel, until it started moving, vibrating, as if the sands were trying to free themselves from the gel's hold.

And then the gel moved, "dancing" as Peter called it. Mesmerized, he stared at the moving gel and he made out the shape of two men in horseback, in full armor and holding swords, fighting. He could almost hear the clang of the swords as they got in contact with each other.

The fight ensued, the men backing and advancing, no one wanting to give up, until one of the men drove his sword on the other man's neck, and the latter fell off his horse. Right after this, the dance stopped and the sand and gel fell on the white handkerchief, the dream going back to its solid gel form, rolling away from the sand.

"I'm sure The Scientist would like to see that," it was Nicolas. They did not see him come back to the room.

"He would?" Peter's face brightened up.

Nicolas nodded, and then said. "We are ready to start. Peter and Chloey, follow me."

"This is it!" Peter could not contain his excitement. Meanwhile, Chloey was silent, serious.

"Good luck!" he said to her. "You can do this."

She gave him a tight smile, and then said before standing up to leave. "See you later."

The three disappeared, and he was left alone in the room. He stood up from the couch and looked around the room, peering at the machinery that all looked foreign to him.

One cabinet caught his attention. It was a glass cabinet, but around it was metal grills, and there was a heavy lock that prevented anyone access to the content—bottles and bottles of dreams that varied in shades of black, red, purple, dark blue, dark green, or a combination of these colors, the most valued kinds of dreams in their world. The darker the color, the higher the value of the dream. Many of these were all a similar shade, but for some reason none of them looked the same. Each one had a unique sheen, a unique glow as it was hit by what little light was in the room.

He continued to look around, mesmerized by the dreams and by all the machinery that he did not notice Nicolas come back in the room after about 30 minutes.

"We are ready for you."

He followed the man to the other room, this one with more lighting than the previous one but with less equipment. There was a table and a chair at the center of the room, and on the table were several bottles of dreams and some paraphernalia. On one end of the room was an area enclosed by a heavy curtain, and beside it a door leading to another room.

Peter and Chloey emerged through the said door. Peter was looking exhausted while Chloey had a different glow in his eyes.

"Hey, are you okay?" he greeted the two, a look of concern in his eyes. "Did you make it alright?"

"Yeah," Chloey nodded. "We did fine." He noticed the colors in her hands were stronger than usual. It was the same with Peter, who was the one silent at the time, looking thoughtful.

"You may stay in the other room to watch," said Nicolas.

On one side of the room, the wall adjacent to the room where the two children came from, was a big mirror, which he recognized as a two-way mirror. He wondered whether there were other people watching on the other side.

As Peter and Chloey disappeared into the other room, he was surprised to see Gregory emerge from the said room; he thought the man would be overseeing the group testing with Victor. However, his biggest surprise came when he saw the next person to emerge from the room, following Gregory.

Chapter 18

He was wearing a white robe similar to the one worn by Nicolas. He had the same three-dotted triangle tattoo as everyone else, but his was similar to Gregory—the two lower dots were bigger than the upper single dot. Alec knew it was his brother the moment Abe walked into the room, felt it even before he saw him. Or perhaps right from the beginning, he had always known the Scientist was Abe.

"Finally, you are here," Gregory addressed Alec.

"Will you be the one overseeing the test?" he asked Gregory, his eyes fixed on Abe.

"No," Gregory answered. "I am here to assist. Abraham and Nicolas will conduct the test."

Abe looked straight at Alec, and for a flitting moment he thought he saw a look of concern on his brother's face, before he pursed his lips and assumed a straight look, not betraying any emotion. "Welcome to your test. My name is Abraham, and I will be conducting the test together with Nicolas. Please take a seat," he gestured at the chair in the middle of the room.

Alec walked towards it and took his seat, all the while looking at Abe, trying to read any emotion from his eyes. He got nothing.

On the table were two pairs of eyeglasses. Nicolas took the first one and wore it. Abe wore the second one. As far as he could remember, Abe never used any glasses throughout his life.

"Please place your hands on the table," Abe said, and he placed both hands with the palms facing up.

Both Abe and Nicolas pressed a tiny button on the right side of their eyeglasses' frame, and Alec saw the lenses change in color.

Abe took a closer look of Alec's hands, touching the tips of his fingers. "Red, yellow, and green, fascinating," he observed.

"You can see the colors in my hands?" Alec asked.

"Yes," Abe nodded, still focused on his fingers. "I designed these specialized glasses specifically for that. You have strong colors in your fingers."

Nicolas took a notepad that was on the table, then a pen, and scribbled some notes on the pad. He then took another seat on the opposite side of the table and started asking question while Abe continued to check his hands.

"You're a Roy," Nicolas said. "Most people who have your abilities inherit them from a family member. Was it the same for you?"

He looked at his brother, who stared back at him with a meaningful look. He answered Nicolas.

"My mother. She was like me, and she taught me everything I needed to know about this… Ability."

"I see," said the man, again scribbling something on his notepad. "Tell me about your family."

A quick flash of his parents lying on their bed surrounded by their own blood quickly ran through his head, and for a moment he could not speak. He looked at Abe again, who did not look back at him, and then he looked at Nicolas, who was waiting for him to answer.

"I am the youngest child; I have a brother," he felt Abe held his breath for a quick moment while examining his hands when he uttered those words, but he did not look at him. "My parents are both dead. They died when I was younger."

"How did they die?"

He was silent, trying to suppress the voices that automatically surfaced inside his head the moment he heard the question. *You killed them*, the voices said to him.

I killed them, he almost uttered the words, before he caught himself.

"They died during a dream transfer."

"To you?" Nicolas asked.

He nodded. "Yes. Some men came into our home right as the dream transfer was happening, and they took the dream. I did not know what happened because I passed out, but when I regained my consciousness both of my parents were dead."

Abe stopped examining his hands and went to another table, busying himself with something.

"And your brother?" Nicolas continued.

"He wasn't there. He had started college at the time and was staying at the university."

"I see," Nicolas looked thoughtful as he scribbled notes on his pad. "You're a Roy, and we know that Roys did not lose the ability to dream like everyone did. Some Roys also have special gifts—do you have any?"

He shook his head. "Not that I am aware of."

"It might be so," said Nicolas. "But tell me about the first Maku encounter you had, with the girl who had the same ability as you."

"Is she here?" he asked. "Is she okay?"

Nicolas stared at him without answering his question, and by his look he did not intend to.

Alec fidgeted in his seat, but then continued. "The girl was like me, yes, but the colors in her hand were darker. The first time I saw her, I found her holding Grace's wrist, and Grace was shouting in pain—she was being tortured."

"Tortured?" asked Nicolas. "What was the girl doing to her?"

"She was holding her wrist, and Grace was in terrible shape. It was clear the girl was doing something to her. Grace was lying on the floor, and she was shaking. I remember her lips turning blue when I found her."

"You managed to save her," Nicolas commented, waiting for something more.

"Yes… I pushed the girl away, and then I checked on Grace. But just the next moment, the girl's hands were around my neck. She was trying to choke me, and her hands were burning." He touched his neck, which had healed by then, although he could still feel the burnt skin that had started to peel away.

"How did you save yourself?"

"I… I didn't. I mean, I am not sure," he tried to remember what happened, but it was all hazy in his mind. "I grabbed the girl's hands, trying to pry it away from my neck. And maybe it was adrenaline, but I felt my hands growing warm, and then… Then everything happened so fast."

"Can you tell us what you remember?" Nicolas prodded.

"I remember images of the girl flashing in my head, very quickly," he explained. "Her memories, I think. And then everything around me seemed to have disappeared, and I was inside the girl's head… I do not really know how it happened."

"Try," said Nicolas. "This will help us understand you, maybe help you, and maybe help the girl, too. And Grace."

"They're both here?" he looked at Nicolas, eyes hopeful.

Nicolas nodded. "Continue."

He exhaled, willing himself to recall everything that happened. "I don't really understand it, but I was inside the girl's head. I could see and hear her thoughts. I could not control it; it felt like I was absorbing her memories, taking them from her."

"Taking them?" Nicolas' eyes were wide with interest, and his brows furrowed.

"Yes, and I could not do anything about it. The memories felt like water, and they kept flowing towards me, until there was nothing more left in the girl. It was so overwhelming that I passed out."

Nicolas nodded, and he could not read the expression in his eyes. He continued scribbling notes on his pad.

"Has anything like this happened to you before?" It was Abe, who approached and once again started examining his hands.

"No," he answered. "That was the first time. And I do not know what to do with these memories."

"What memories?" Abe looked at him, an uncertain look in his eyes.

"They're in me. And not as second-hand memories," he explained. "I experience them as the Maku girl. In these memories I become her. The memories come and go, and I cannot control them."

"Are you telling me that you took the girl's memory?" Nicolas asked.

"I think so, but not intentionally. I do not want these memories."

"That is certainly something we have not heard of," Nicolas looked at Abe, who was looking at him at the time. "Should we test that?"

Abe looked deep in thought, before saying. "Definitely, but let us start with something simpler." He opened a small cabinet and took a bottle out of it—a yellow dream. "Have you tried ingesting dreams before?" Abe asked. "Apart from yours, of course."

He shook his head. "No."

"Do you know what happens when a person consumes a dream that isn't his?"

He stared at his brother, searching his eyes, remembering the time when they found him passed out from ingesting a dream. He wondered whether Abe remembered that. He nodded his head. "Yes. I have seen people do that, and around my neighborhood there were so many people with green veins in their eyes from being addicted to dreams."

"A dream might give someone a new experience, and they get temporary high from the novelty of that experience," explained Abe, giving the bottle a shake. "But, every time they ingest a dream that isn't theirs, their soul is stripped away little by little, until nothing is left."

"Or..." added Nicolas. "When the dream is so much heavier than their mind can handle, they lose their sanity entirely, or their soul, and some die."

"Are you comfortable in your chair?" asked Abe. He poured the yellow gel on his open right palm. "I want you to take this dream. It is yellow, safe enough for someone who has never done it before."

He hesitated, looking at the dream on his palm.

"Anytime you're ready," said Abe.

He leaned back on his chair, and then with the dream clasped in his right hand, he pressed his right wrist. Almost instantly, he felt the cool gel dry up on his palm as it got easily absorbed through his skin.

The room started to blur, and before long he found himself in what looked like to be an open stadium—in the middle of a baseball field. He was drowning in the noise of all the people around, watching and cheering for the players. He was holding a baseball bat, and the pitcher was getting ready to throw the ball. And then finally he did, and his full attention zoomed in on the ball. He could almost hear it whiz by as it approached, and he swung the bat with all his strength.

The moment the bat met the ball, he blinked and everything seemed to play rewind in a flash. The next moment, he was outside of the dream and all he could see was the yellow gel, magnified a hundred times in front of him, and he could see the entire scene right there, trapped in that one moment, and everything existing like a world, a scene, captured inside the yellow gel. He touched the gel, and the soft surface reacted to the pressure from his finger, creating a ripple that reverberated across the gel's surface. He moved the gel, slowly rotating it like a globe, looking at the dream from different perspectives—from the pitcher's side, the batter's side, zooming in on the crowd cheering. He touched the gel, and soon it shrunk until it was back to its original size on his palm, and he opened his eyes to find himself back in the room, sitting on the chair.

Chapter 19

He opened his palm and saw the dream right there, even brighter than it was before.

Abe took a closer look at it. "What happened?" he asked, examining the gel.

"I... I was in the dream, and then I was outside of it," he explained, his own curiosity growing.

"What do you mean outside of it?" Abe looked at him, peering at his eyes.

"I was out of the dream; I could see it from different angles."

"You were not in the dream?"

"No, I was. I mean, in the beginning. And then I was outside of it, outside of the yellow bubble, and the dream was frozen and I could observe it."

Abe continued searching his eyes. "There are no green veins, no evidence of a dream ingestion," he observed. "The symptoms usually occur the first time you ingest a dream, and most people end up nauseous after. Do you feel anything different?"

He blinked a few times, and then shook his head. "No, I don't feel anything different."

Abe nodded, and then he looked at Gregory, who took it as a signal and occupied the chair in front of him. He took a bottle of dreams from his pocket, a red gel inside it, and then handed the bottle to Abe.

"This is strong enough?" Abe asked, peering at the bottle against the fluorescent light in the room.

"Yes," Gregory answered, looking straight at Alec with no expression on his face.

"Okay," he handed the bottle back to Gregory, and then turned to him. "We'll see how you do when a dream is passed on to you directly from someone who is not closely related to you—that means no blood relation."

"A dream transfer. But we are not related. Isn't that… Prohibited?" he asked.

"Of course it is," answered Abe. "It can potentially harm a person, even more than ingesting a dream in gel form. When you ingest a gel dream that isn't yours, you only have the dream to handle—how potent it is and how it will affect your mind. When a dream is passed on to you by another person, someone not related to you, you must handle not just the dream but the person passing it on to you—the person's intent, how the transfer happens, a lot of variables that almost always lead to trouble. But Gregory has done this several times. He's learned restraint, and he'll know how to control the transfer, so you should have no problem on that end. Still, be ready for anything. We never know how your mind will react."

He looked at Gregory once again, but the absence of expression on his face did not give him any consolation.

"Are you ready?" Abe asked.

He nodded his head. "Yes."

Gregory poured the content of the bottle on his own palm, a red dream, a stronger one. He then closed his palm and pressed on his wrist, closing his eyes. When he opened his palms again, the dream was gone.

And then Gregory opened his eyes, a glazed expression reflected on them. It took a few moments before the look of clarity was back in his eyes, and he opened and closed his palm.

"Are you okay?" Abe asked.

"Yes," Gregory answered, quiet. The dream was swimming inside his head, and he felt half of him was in the room and the other half was inside his head. The many instances he had done the exercise was helping him stay calm while being in two worlds at once.

"And you?" Abe looked at Alec.

"Yes," he nodded.

Gregory took his palm, almost like a handshake. And then he pressed on Alec's wrist. Alec started feeling a sensation of warmth in his head, at the roots of his hair, and he closed his eyes as a barrage of red images flashed in his mind, a red dream taking form.

He found himself in the middle of a store, and he was holding a gun.

"Greg! Here!" A man in a mask shoved a backpack at him before running behind a cabinet, and he realized he was wearing a mask, too. He opened the backpack and saw a transparent box inside, filled with bottles of dreams of different colors.

At the counter, another man in a similar mask was taking money from the counter, shoving everything inside a duffle bag.

"No!" a shout came from the back of the store.

"Greg! Come here!" a man called for him.

He ran to the back of the store to find the first man in a mask, together with an older man slumped on the floor, a fearful look reflected on his face and blood beside his mouth.

"This man wouldn't tell me where the key to that cabinet is," the man complained, anger evident in his voice, as he gestured towards a metal cabinet.

"Please, don't," the man pleaded. "It's my family's dreams. I've given you all the other bottles in this store, but not my family's dreams. Please."

"Where's the key?!" the other man shouted. "This is the last time I ask you."

"No," the man continued to plead. "Please."

"Greg," the other man called, and he approached the older man, kneeling beside him on the floor.

"You really should give us the key," he said to the man, placing the gun on a chair nearby. "It's not worth your life."

He removed the glove he had on his hands, to reveal colored fingers—a dark blue and dark red hue. He grabbed the man's shoulder, and almost instantly the man's whole body shook and he smelled burning flesh.

"No! No! Don't!" he heard himself shouting, only to realize that the shouting was only in his head. He was still grabbing the man's shoulder, and the man's body was still shaking.

"No! No!" he repeated, willing his hands, Gregory's hands, to get off the man's shoulder. "Stooop!"

A series of images flashed through his head, the time in the dream moving backward and then forward, and the next moment he was once again outside of the dream. In front of him was the dream gel, magnified a hundred times, and everyone inside it a statue caught in time—the man's body no longer shaking but the fear still reflected in his eyes, Gregory with an intense look in his eyes behind the mask, and the other man standing close holding a gun.

And then the world inside the gel resumed as he watched outside it. The man continued shaking as the colors in Gregory's fingers glowed brighter.

"Tell us where the key is!" shouted the other man in a mask, but the old man could not hear him. His body convulsed and blood started oozing out of his nose.

"Greg! Stop! Stop!" shouted the other man. "You're killing him!"

Greg did not seem to hear him. His eyes were glazed, and he looked like he was not there—he was caught up inside his head, inside the man's head.

The man's body stopped moving, and smoke was rising from the skin on his shoulders where Gregory was grabbing him.

And then there was a commotion at the door.

"League of the Dream Hunters!" he heard someone shout, and then a bullet whizzed by, hitting Gregory on the arms.

Everything darkened, inside the dream and around him. The next moment, he was back in the room clasping the red gel in his palm.

Gregory was panting, still reeling from the dream, and he was looking at him with questions in his eyes.

"How did you do that?" Gregory asked.

"What happened?" came another question from Abe.

"You went outside of it," Gregory said, a mixture of confusion and amazement in his voice.

"That was… You were…" Alec could not find the will to say the words as he remembered what happened. He was panting, trying to catch his breath. "It was not a dream. It was a memory, wasn't it?"

Gregory looked past him, remembering that single moment ages ago. "Yes, it is a memory that has haunted me ever since that day."

"You killed the man," it was a statement. "We are the same, you and me. Why didn't you tell me?"

Gregory shook his head, a look of regret in his eyes. "It's not something to be proud of."

He took the empty glass bottle and gestured for Alec to pour the red substance back from his palm, which he did.

"You went outside of it," said Abe. "What does that mean?"

"Just like the first time," he explained. "I was in the dream, or the memory, and then I was outside of it; I was observing everything from outside the bubble."

He could see Nicolas scribbling on his pad, a look of concentration on his face. Every now and then, he would look at him, trying to read his eyes and gestures as he spoke.

"How did you do it?" asked Abe. "Did anything trigger it? Was it at will?"

"No. I don't know. There was no trigger," he tried to recall the memory. "It just happened when I tried reacting to it, telling Gregory—myself—to stop. I think my reaction triggered the separation."

"A separation in personality," Abe said, in a voice so low it seemed like he was talking to himself, and then he asked. "And this is the first time this happened to you? In a dream or a memory?"

He nodded. "The first dream, the yellow dream earlier, in the baseball field. That was the first time."

Abe looked at Gregory, and the two exchanged a meaningful look, before Abe went to the other room and Gregory followed. He followed them with his eyes.

"Am I done with the test?" he asked Nicolas. "Are they deciding now whether I passed?"

What if he doesn't? What if the things he did were not supposed to be done? What if it wasn't the right reaction to a dream?

He had a lot of questions. He wanted to understand what happened in the dream. He also wanted to understand what Abe was doing in the league, and why he had to disappear. And what if he failed the test?

Chapter 20

As he was trying to grasp at an answer to his questions, Abe and Gregory came back in the room.

"For the last part of the test, we want you to try something," declared Abe. He went to the curtained part of the room and pulled the curtain back, revealing a hospital bed with someone in it.

He slowly approached the bed and was shocked to find Grace there, almost all her exposed skin covered in splotches of white, including her hair. She was asleep, with several medical equipment connected to her body, monitoring her vital signs.

"What happened to her?" he asked. Grace looked pale; her eyes closed. One of her hands were bandaged where the Maku girl touched her, while the other hand was healing.

"We don't know," answered Abe. Ever since he was brought here, she had been unwell. She would wake up now and then, but she would mostly sleep."

Abe took a small penlight from his coat pocket and opened Grace's eyes with his fingers, shining the light on them. He saw green veins across the surface of the whites of her eyes. Grace stirred in her sleep but did not completely wake up.

"The veins in her eyes, is that a side effect, too?" he asked Abe.

"No," Abe shook his head. "We have been giving her small doses of dreams, to see if that would stimulate her mind. But so far, we have not made much progress."

"What do you want me to do?"

"Do you remember the Maku girl?" asked Abe. "You had the same effect on her, the way she had that effect on Grace?"

"Yes, I think so. Is the girl, okay?"

"She'll live," was what Abe simply said. "But Grace— you think you can reverse the effect on her?"

"Reverse? What do you mean?"

"You said you had the girl's memory," Abe explained. "That you involuntarily took some of them. We think the girl might have taken Grace's memory, too. And it is likely worse with her, because it seemed intentional—the girl knew what she was doing."

He nodded understanding.

"You want me to give some memories back to Grace? Will I steal her memories back from the Maku girl?" his voice sounded apprehensive.

"No, no," Abe countered. "We can't risk you entering the mind of the Maku girl right now. She is too unstable, too emotional, and we have not determined what she is fully capable of."

"Then… What can I do?"

Abe looked at Gregory, hesitation in his eyes.

"We want you to just try and go there," Gregory answered. "See what memories you find in Grace. Do you have memories of her? Or dreams. That might be better."

"I have no dreams of her, but I have some memories," he said, recalling the first time they met.

"If that's all you have, then we work with that," declared Gregory.

"It might be too risky," Abe finally said. "Dreams we can handle, but memories are something we haven't really explored."

"You've seen his capability," Gregory countered. "No one who had been in this room has that."

He stared at Gregory, remembering the memory. "You can do that, too," he blurted out, and then he realized the tone of accusation in his voice. "In the dream, with the old man…" He stopped talking as Gregory's face turned dark and grim.

"Don't think we didn't try," Gregory said quietly. "I haven't been able to reach her. You might be her best chance right now."

He was silent for a moment, and then he nodded, with resolve in his eyes. "I'll do it."

He felt and heard Abe exhale a deep sigh, and they locked eyes without saying a word.

"Okay," Abe said. He gestured for him to take a seat beside Grace's bed, which he did. "Take your time, no pressure. If it works, then good. If it does not, it is okay."

He looked at Grace's face, her eyes closed, most of her face white, and her lips formed into a slight frown. He took her hand, the one without a bandage, and watched as the colors in his fingers enveloped her hands, too. He touched her wrist, unsure whether it worked the same with memories. Before he could try and press her pulse point, however, he felt the first flash of image run in his head, very fast he was not able to capture or understand it.

"Take your time," he heard Abe's voice. "Slow down and breathe. And follow your instinct."

He followed his voice, inhaling a deep breath as more and more images flashed in his mind—Grace with her older brother and younger sister, at the beach; Grace staring at herself in the mirror, behind him a cabinet containing a few bottles of dreams; Grace being bullied in school; her first day of training in the league; and then that memory on the day of the raid of the Maku settlement, as they boarded the truck and they met for the first time.

"Ooh, now he talks," it was Emerson, during the first time they met. "Bet you will be screaming later out there."

"Stop it, Emer," there was a hardness in Grace's voice that he did not notice the first time. *"Don't mind him. He is like that to everyone; thinks he is better than all of us."*

"Oh, you bet I am," was Emerson's comeback.

Wait, he heard his own voice echo all around him, inside Grace's head. The memories stopped moving, his focus locked on that memory of the first day they met at the truck.

He summoned his own memory of that event, until he saw and felt it come to the surface.

"Guys, this is Alec," Carl was introducing him to the group. *"That's Emerson, Wendell, Grace, Hannah, and King,"* he gave each one a closer look. *"Alec is a new recruit."*

"New recruit?!" it was Hannah who spoke. *"What are you doing here?"*

He did not answer. Instead, he scanned the group and looked at Grace, who was quietly listening to the conversation. She was seated across him.

"Grace," he called to her. "Hey."

At first, Grace didn't seem to hear him as she focused on the conversations happening around.

"Grace," he tried again. "It's Alec. This happened in the past—do you remember?"

Grace blinked, appearing to hear him for the first time. And then, everything blurred around them as both of their individual memories combined into one, with both inside both memories, now one.

"Hey," he said to Grace, smiling. "Do you remember this?"

Grace blinked once again, and then her eyes focused on him.

"Alec?" she asked, and then she looked around confused. "What happened?"

"Don't panic, okay?" he said, reassuring her. "I'm in your head, and you're in mine."

"What?" she asked. "What are you saying?"

"This," he gestured all around him, with Emerson and the rest talking, although they could not hear them anymore. "It's our memories. And it is not happening now—we are inside our memories."

"What do you mean?" Grace looked confused.

"Do you remember the raid of the Maku settlement at the desert?" he asked. "The Maku girl?"

"The Maku girl," her eyes widened, and she inadvertently touched her wrist. And then she looked around her as realization dawned on her. "This was before the raid… How did I…?"

"Listen, it's memories," he explained, trying to be as gentle as he could. "We are inside our memories."

Grace looked around her, trying to understand, as voices floated in and out around them as the other league members continued with their excited chitchat.

"Do you remember what happened after the Maku girl attacked you?" he asked.

Grace looked thoughtful as she recalled the events, and he saw a flash of anxiety cross her eyes.

"I remember losing consciousness, and then the next thing I knew I was lying on a bed inside a dimly lit room. I would wake up, but then sleep would pull me back. There was nothing I could do."

"Yes," he tried his best to reassure her. "And do you remember this, the first time we met?"

Grace looked around them once again, her eyes widening at the recollection, and then a confused look crossing her face. "This happened before the Maku attack," she said. "How…?"

"Memories," he answered. "We are in our shared memories."

"What?" Grace had a hard time comprehending everything.

"Right now, you are still lying asleep in the bed, back at the headquarters," he patiently explained. "I went back to our memory to try and talk to you."

"What?" And then look of understanding slowly crossed Grace's eyes. "Oh… How's everyone?"

"We are doing okay, but we are all very worried about you. We want you to get better."

"How?" asked Grace.

"We think that the Maku girl stole some of your memories. Gregory and… The Scientist, they are trying to find a way to bring you back to your consciousness, but we need your help. We need you to push your mind to go back."

Grace was silent, and then she nodded her head. "I want to go back."

He nodded his head, too. "That's good. We are all waiting for you." He got up from the bench he was sitting in in the truck and extended his hand for Grace to take. "C'mon."

Grace took his hand, and they jumped off the truck. The moment his feet touched the ground, everything went dark, and then he woke up back in the room, still holding Grace's hand.

"Alec," Abe was shaking his shoulder. "Alec, are you okay?"

He blinked a few times, and then his environment grew clearer. He stared at Abe for a few seconds, and then he turned his gaze on Grace. She was still asleep, her eyes unmoving, the rise and fall of her chest steady with her breathing. He noticed she wasn't as pale as she was before, but she hadn't woken up. Nicolas was examining her.

"How is she?" he asked, his voice unsteady.

Nicolas answered. "She looks the same, but maybe any effect is not immediately felt."

"What happened?" Gregory asked. "Did you reach her memories?"

He nodded. "Yes. She remembered. I talked to her, asked her to find the will to go back, and she said she would."

Nicolas nodded, while Nicolas scribbled something on his notebook.

"The only thing we can do for now is wait," declared Abe. "Your test is done. Get some rest for now."

"Did I... Did I pass?" he asked.

"We will have to study the data," answered Abe. "We will let you know."

He looked at Abe, but the latter avoided his gaze as he tried sorting out the paraphernalia on the table.

"Let's go," Gregory called, turning towards the door.

He gave Abe one last glance, who turned towards him and gave him a look he could not understand, before turning back to what he was doing.

"Alec!" it was Chloey emerging from the other room, followed by Peter. "You did so well! We were watching you from the other side."

"Hey," he greeted the two children, and they went out of the room together. "How did your tests go?"

"I showed them the dancing sand!" exclaimed Peter, the excitement in his voice evident.

"I think it went okay," Chloey looked thoughtful. "But I didn't like the dream."

"I liked mine," said Peter. "I was in the park and riding the rollercoaster! And then it stopped in the middle and

I was hanging upside down! I was scared at first, and then the rollercoaster started moving, and it was a lot of fun!"

"You're so brave!" he exclaimed, and Peter grinned. "What was yours?" he asked Chloey.

"I was playing with a cat. Her name was Hershey. And then he scratched me," he touched her arm absentmindedly, where she thought the scratch was. "But it was an accident. And then a man came and took her," Chloey frowned. "He put him in a cage. I was telling him the cat was mine, and the scratch did not mean anything, but he would not listen to me." There were tears at the corner of Chloey's eyes as she said this.

"Do you have a pet?" Alec asked.

She shook her head, then said, "I always wanted one, but my mom did not want me to have it. She said it's too much work, and I need to focus…" She looked at her hands, which had colors dancing around them.

"Maybe when you're older, you can have a pet," he patted the girl's head, trying to pacify her.

"That's what I told her!" said Peter. "When we're big like you, or like Gregory," he looked up at the man, who simply smiled back at him. "We can have pets and whatever we like."

They arrived at the bottom of the stairs, and he said goodbye to the twins and Gregory. He searched for his friends and fellow recruits, his mind distracted from the discovery that Abe was indeed with the league and from everything that happened during his test.

Chapter 21

"I knew I would be for combat," Dexter was telling the group. It was two days after they all took the final test. "I can't wait to be out there and actually get into some action."

"What's yours?" Alec asked Wendell, who was busy polishing his blade.

Wendell raised the blade, checking the edges. "This," he said. "Weapons master. I will get to do some training, too."

"You tested upstairs, right? With that non-smiling, serious man in white?" Dexter laughed.

"Nicolas," he explained. "He's apprentice to the Scientist."

"Dream research," Wendell appeared to be considering it, and then said, "Not for me. I would rather do something with my hands."

"And I would rather kill some Makus!" exclaimed Dexter.

"Alec!" it was Chloey approaching them, followed by Peter behind her. Chloey handed her a sealed white envelope. "The Scientist gave this to me. He said to give this only to you."

"He gave it to us!" said Peter, holding his bottle of sand.

"Just me," clarified Chloey. "He said to come see him, about your test."

"Thank you," he stood up, then said to his friends, "See you guys later."

He went to the sleeping quarters, where he knew no one was around at the time, and then opened the envelope. It contained two sets of numbers, 2300 and 936499, and then three words: "Don't tell anyone."

Did he mean to meet at 11:00 PM that day? And what does the other set of numbers mean? And then he remembered something.

That same day at 11:00 PM, when the headquarters have quieted and most of his fellow recruits were asleep, he got up from his bed, arranged his pillows and blanket so it would look like he was sleeping under the covers, took his shoes from under the bed, and slowly crept out of the room.

Save for some far-off noise somewhere in the training hall, everything appeared to have settled in for the night. It was five minutes before 11 when he got up; he had enough time to spare to ensure he reached the dream room without alerting anyone and without anyone noticing anything amiss.

He reached the bottom of the metal stairs, and he was startled to hear the creaking amid the quiet of the night. The metal would creak with every step, and after taking about six to seven steps up, he heard two voices in conversation, getting closer and closer.

He stayed where he was, hiding in the shadows and holding his breath, as the two men passed underneath him. He recognized one of them to be the man he first saw on the tunnel when he came to the league the first time, following Gregory. He was talking to another man.

"I trust you have been briefed about this shipment?" the familiar man was asking.

"Yes," the other man answered. "Shipment coming in every Tuesday, after midnight."

"Yes" the first man confirmed. "It should be here in a couple of hours."

"How many bottles?"

"I'm not sure," answered the first man. "Maybe in the hundreds, and I heard there are some black ones in this batch."

When he was sure the men had passed and were far enough, he continued to slowly climb the stairs, stopping every time he thought the creaking of the metal was echoing all around him, waiting for the sound to settle down.

He arrived in the hallway and walked the short distance to the door, punching in the series of numbers from the note he received from Abe into the keypad. Somewhere on the other side of the door something clicked, and then it opened.

The room was dim, but the door to the next room showed the light was open in the other room where he took his test. He slowly went to the other room, but no one was there. When he looked towards the corner where Grace was the previous time, he found the curtain parted and the bed empty. Grace was not there.

"I'm in here," he heard his brother's voice from the observation room where Chloey and Peter stayed the previous time to watch him. He went there to find his brother, Abe, sitting on a chair, with a pen and notepad on a table in front of him.

"Close the door," he said quietly. And then as soon as he did, Abe asked, "What are you doing here?"

"You disappeared," he answered, occupying the other chair. He stared at his brother and he noticed the tired look on his face, hair disheveled and dark circles under his eyes. He didn't notice it the first time. "I was trying to find you."

"You shouldn't have come here; this is the last place you should be," Abe buried his face in his hands.

"Why did you have to leave, and without a trace?" his voice was laced with accusation. "You could have told me you were part of the league. I would have understood."

"No, you won't," he said. "The reason I disappeared was to protect you."

"What? What do you mean protect me?"

"I have always been envious of you when we were growing up," Abe said. "I never once considered how difficult it must have been for you to try and understand your gift and to adjust to all of it. I was blinded by my jealousy of the relationship you and mom had. It's not always a gift, though, is it? It is a curse, too."

"What are you talking about?" he asked, confused.

Abe stood up and walked to a small cabinet, and that's when he noticed it—one of his brother's feet had a metal collar around the ankle, and there was a blinking button on it.

"What is that?" he asked, suddenly worried. "Why do you have an ankle monitor?"

Abe took a few bottles of dreams from the cabinet, closed the cabinet door, and then went back and sit down on the chair, carefully lining up the bottles on the table, just like he used to do with his own bottles of dreams back at their home.

He sat back down, and then turned to face him. "The league isn't what you think it is."

"What does that mean? Are they the ones who did this to you?" he gestured at his brother's feet.

"I joined the league about a year ago, thinking I could expand my work and research on dreams, imagining I would be able to do some good," his brother said. "What a foolish idea!"

He looked at him without saying a word, not understanding what he was talking about.

"Remember mom's stolen dream?" Abe asked, a look of wildness in his eyes.

The images once again flashed across his head. The dream transfer. He could almost hear his mom's voice. "I am passing this on to you. It is now yours, and you will carry with it the stories of your great, great grandparents." And then his mom and dad sprawled on the bed, surrounded by their own blood.

"The dream that killed them," he whispered.

"It wasn't the dream that killed them," Abe said. "It was the league."

"What?" his mouth fell upon hearing his brother's statement. "How?"

"They are behind all of it," Abe's voice was hard. "They knew about mom, had her targeted for her ability. And so are other people like her. You... It is just a matter of time for you."

"They're not what we all know them to be?" he asked.

"On the opposite," said his brother. "They are behind all the robbery, all the dreams disappearing."

"But... How did you know all these? Is that the reason you're..." he looked at his brother's feet.

Abe nodded. "They suspect, but they can't kill me. I am too valuable to them, and no one has managed to understand my research or replicate my methods. But it's only a matter of time for me, too. Once Nicolas learns everything, I will be of no value to the league."

"Who else knows about this?" he asked, thinking about all the people he knew in the league. "Is everyone here a part of it?"

"No," Abe shook his head. "Many league members believe they are here for a good cause, but the leaders knew, together with several members."

"Gregory?" he asked, thinking about the man's-colored fingers and hands.

Abe gave another shake of the head. "I'm not sure, but I wouldn't trust him—he works closely with Victor, and I wouldn't be surprised if Victor is a part of all of it. He's leader of the combat team, after all.

"We can take all the dreams back, and then disappear," he volunteered.

"Disappear?" Abe asked. "You think it will be easier to disappear, especially now that you are here? They will not let you go just like that."

"Why not? People need to know the truth, if they are really behind all the stolen dreams—we can expose the league."

"Do you know what you are?" Abe looked at him straight in the eyes. "You're a vessel, and you will be very valuable to the league, maybe even more than me, the moment they realize that."

"What is a vessel?" he asked.

"Someone who can hold and control dreams in their head. And not only dreams, but thoughts, memories," Abe looked worried. "I disappeared to protect you, when I found out what the league was about. I did not want what happened to Mom to also happen to you."

He was baffled by all the revelation; everything was new to him, too. "Mom," he asked. "Was she like me? Did she pass this on to me?"

Abe shook his head. "I don't know. I always knew you and mom had something different, but that you were special—Mom always said that. I thought it was because you were her favorite," his brother grew silent, looking down on the floor. "I did not realize… She might have seen all these before, known these all about you. And I wish I'd known before, about you, about her. I might have helped them—and you—before all of these happened."

He was silent, too, pondering on what his brother revealed, how he felt everything he was feeling, too, about their parents' death—all the guilt and remorse.

"I'm sorry," he said. "Mom loved you just the way he loved me. And dad, too."

Abe nodded. "I know. It just took me a while to accept that even though they loved us differently, it was loving all the same. And I won't let anything bad happen to you. I promised Mom that."

"What will they do with me?" he asked.

"I don't think they are aware about what you can actually do," Abe said. "Except Nicolas and Gregory. The moment they understand what you're capable of, they won't let you go. We must find a way to get you out before that happens."

"How about Chloey? And Peter? They're like me, too. Will the league harm them? They are just kids."

"I don't think they will," Abe answered. "At least not yet. But you cannot trust the people around you—we don't know who's with the league and who's not. You must get out of here."

"I can't, not without you," he said. "And if the missing dream is here, we must find it. We cannot leave without it."

Abe was silent for a moment before turning to him. "Give me a bit more time to plan our next steps. For now, you will pass the test. The leaders would want you examined and trained right away, but you need to make sure they don't find out about your full capability. Otherwise, it would be harder for me to get you out."

He nodded, most of his brother's words he was still trying to grasp at.

"How do we find the dream? Can you even go out of this room?" he asked. "Let me help you. Tell me what I can do to help."

Abe stared at him, a momentary look of fondness in his eyes, before they turned hard and serious.

"Okay, but for now I need you to just be a recruit. Don't attract any unnecessary attention while I make plans. I will let you know what we must do next."

He nodded.

"It's time for you to go, before someone else finds out you're not in your bunk," said Abe, getting up from the chair. "Take care of yourself, and don't let anyone find out."

He nodded once again, not knowing what to say. And then he was surprised when his brother gave him a quick hug, tapping him on the back as he did. He hugged him back awkwardly, feeling an unexpected sense of relief as he did.

"I'm so glad I found you," he uttered sheepishly, before turning away to leave.

"Me, too," his brother said, looking as awkward as he did. "I will see you again soon."

Chapter 22

"They all need to die; they deserve it," Emerson was telling the group. He arrived at the dining room with everyone seated together—the first friends he met from the league during his first day and the friends he met during training, fellow recruits who had become his buddies and companions.

"Where'd you been?" asked King, unable to clearly enunciate his question with his mouth full of food. The guy moved to give him sitting space.

"Training," he answered. After the conversation with Abe, he'd been training with Nicolas and the twins, and he'd never seen his brother again except during occasional moments when he'd come out of the other room while they were training in the dream room. During those times, he would not be wearing the ankle monitor, and he wouldn't give any acknowledgment to him or to the kids except for a brief, expressionless, uninterested glance.

"No, man," countered Carl. "If we are trying to cure the Makus, we shouldn't be killing them."

"But we're not killing everyone," it was Wendell who added. "Only the hopeless cases. The old Makus, there is no possible cure for them. They will only cause trouble. And in fact, they already have. They have the highest dream consumption."

He looked around at the table, curious about the discussion.

"What happened?" he asked Hannah, who was seated across him.

"They just came from a raid of another Maku settlement. Everyone died."

"Everyone?"

"Not everyone," protested Wendell. "They brought in one Maku boy."

"Hundreds, man!" Carl sounded exasperated. "And it wasn't a raid. It was a massacre—did you see how no one had any weapon, how the Makus looked helpless, and how everyone just shot at everyone? There was no justice there."

"Oh, c'mon," Emerson interrupted. "You're talking about justice? These Makus kill, rob, and they're not even humans—they're monsters. Did you see them?"

"They're humans underneath," Mikhail backed Carl. "And that's why we are curing them, because they are still humans."

"Some Makus, yes," added King. "But most of them are monsters and will not hesitate to kill if they have to."

"Enough, guys," it was Jared. "We follow orders. We do what must be done, because only us can do that. No one else."

Emerson shrugged, a look of gloating in his eyes. "See? Orders."

Carl shook his head, still unconvinced.

"Hey guys," everyone turned at the familiar voice.

"Grace!" exclaimed Mikhail. She was standing there, looking all better and back to normal, although her hair had remained white.

Everyone stood to hug or give Grace a pat on the shoulders, and they moved to give her space beside him.

"Cool hair!" teased Hannah. "Are you okay?"

Grace nodded. "Yeah, save for some souvenir from the encounter." She raised her hands to reveal scars and some minor wounds that have not yet fully healed from the Maku girl grabbing her hands.

She turned her attention to him. "I saw you, in that truck."

He smiled. "You remember?"

"Yeah, it was surreal," her eyes took on a reminiscent look. "To be in a dream, part of it, and then outside of it examining the dream. I think it helped me remember that I can get out and go back, wake up. How did you do that?"

He shook his head while shrugging his shoulders. "It's something new I'm discovering, too. Everything is, just… I am learning a lot of things about me and about the league."

"Do you know which group you'll join?" asked King, looking at Grace.

"I was asked to consider and try the test for being a Gatherer," she answered. "Although I am also interested in combat. They are giving me time to fully recuperate."

He looked around at his quiet surroundings. Seeing no one was there, he quietly punched the numbers on the keypad right by the door until the door opened and he slid behind it, finding himself in the dream room. He'd been here a few times ever since that first conversation with his brother, and they'd talked about the next steps to take to escape and sabotage the league's plans.

"Some of the dreams are right here in this room, but most of these are in the storage room," explained Abe. "I have had no access to that room ever since I first came here, but it's found on the left side of the headquarters."

He remembered the conversation he heard between the two men below the stairs when he first came to see his brother.

"There is a shipment that comes in every Tuesday after midnight," he said. "The shipment is probably brought there, in the storage room."

"That's right," Abe stroked his chin, trying to think. "If you can find the storage room, that's where all the stolen dreams will be."

"How many bottles are we talking about?" he asked. "If it's a weekly shipment, chances are there may be hundreds, maybe thousands of bottles, already there. We cannot possibly take all of that."

"We're not taking everything," said Abe. "It's impossible. But there should be a glass safe in there that has the prized collection of the league. These are the most valuable dreams, and these are the same dreams they are experimenting on. I have only seen this case, but I have never had a chance to examine the contents."

Abe had mentioned about the different experiments the league was doing. Worse than dream conjuring or ingestion, they are also working on dream manipulation, which includes processes like cloning, as well as dream deconstruction and reconstruction, trying to create higher-value synthetic dreams for black market trading and selling.

"Without these dreams, the league will not be able to go through many of the experiments they are doing," Abe continued. "I know of other dream scientists across the country, some of them also working for the league. I must reach out to them once we find our way out of here; we need their help to expose the league and put an end to all of these."

"I can find the storage room and take the dreams," he volunteered. "I will need a few days to do it." A shipment was coming a few days away, and it was his key to the storage room.

Abe was silent, and then he slowly nodded. "Be careful. I will start working on some plans to keep us safe once we are out of here."

"Are you ready?"

He found himself in the same room a couple of days after the last conversation with Abe, but this time he was there in the morning, with Chloey and Peter, and with Nicolas. Abe was nowhere in sight.

They have started training with Nicolas, starting with the basics of dream handling.

"Yes, we're ready," answered Peter, excitement evident in his voice.

Chloey was holding a blue gel in her left hand, and her right hand was ready to press on her left wrist.

"Okay, Chloey, slowly…" reminded Nicolas.

Chloey pressed on the pulse point on her wrist, and the gel slowly disappeared into her palm. Her eyes took on a glazed look.

"Can you hear me?" asked Nicolas.

Chloey did not answer, as she slowly closed her eyes.

"Chloey," called Nicolas once again. "Listen to me."

After a few moments, Chloey once again opened her eyes.

"Do you hear me now?" again, Nicolas asked.

Chloey nodded.

"Okay, very good. It is time to pass the dream to Peter."

Chloey took Peter's hands, looking half immersed in her dreams and half aware of her surroundings. She pressed on Peter's wrist.

"Slowly, slowly," reminded Nicolas.

Peter's eyes started taking on a glazed look, too, and soon he was lost in the dream.

"Peter," called Nicolas. "Can you hear me?"

No answer came.

"Peter," again Nicolas called, but Peter still did not answer.

Chloey slowly returned to her present surroundings, and Nicolas said to her in a whisper, "Good job."

Chloey smiled, and then focused her attention to Peter.

"Can you hear me, Peter?" Nicolas asked again, and again Peter did not answer.

After a while, they saw the blue gel slowly appearing on his palms, and then Peter slowly woke up. He focused his eyes on his surroundings, and then looked at Chloey. "Your dream was weird," he said. "I was walking in a field of flowers and they were singing to me. Weird. You should have chosen something fun."

"But it was fun," defended Chloey. "It's more fun than your scary dreams."

"Did you hear my voice while you were dreaming?" asked Nicolas.

Peter turned to him. "I think I did, but it was very faint. And all those flowers singing, ugh!" he frowned in exaggeration.

"Okay, that's a good start," said Nicolas. "We will try it again later, and then I want you to focus on my voice when you hear it, okay?"

Peter nodded. "Okay. But please choose another dream," he addressed this one to Chloey, who rolled her eyes at him in a childish way.

"I'll be back for you," Nicolas turned to him, before heading to the other room.

"You did a great job," he told the twins when Nicolas was gone.

"You need to listen more," Chloey turned to Peter. "Like Mariel told us."

"I can do it," answered Peter. "If you choose a fun dream, it will be easier."

"Who's Mariel?" he asked.

"She's our friend," it was Chloey who answered. "She's a Roy, too."

"And Robin, and Zee," added Peter.

"They're all your friends? They're here?"

"Yeah," said Chloey. "Mariel had been helping us practice."

"But they can't train with us," said Peter. "They are locked in their room and can't go out."

"Wait," he said, a hint of alarm creeping up in his voice. "Are they the Makus that were brought in?"

Peter nodded, his eyes widening.

"Peter!" Chloey exclaimed. "We're not supposed to tell!"

"But it's Alec," Peter countered in a whiny voice. "He's, our friend."

Chloey appeared to think for a bit, before conceding.

"Fine," she finally said. "But do not tell anyone," She added in a lower voice. "We're not supposed to talk to them."

"Yeah, you shouldn't," he agreed, sounding worried. "They're dangerous."

"They're friendly," said Peter. "Just bored, and they miss their family. Mariel would often cry."

"They are nice," Chloey added. "They showed us some tricks, and they are teaching us how to control our dreams."

"You should meet them!" there was excitement in Peter's voice. "They can teach you, too."

"I don't know," he remembered the Maku girl, both the fear and hatred in her eyes. "They might not like to meet an adult."

"We will tell them you want to meet them," said Peter. "And if they want to, we can take you."

He considered the offer for a moment, and then he remembered the plans he had with Abe. The girl might give him more clarity and answers. "Okay," he finally said.

Chapter 23

"Three boxes," said one of the two men he saw below the stairs a few days ago. They were accompanied by another man who carried a pistol slung on his right shoulder, and they were in another entrance to the headquarters. He followed the three men, hiding in the shadows and keeping his footsteps as light as possible.

Three other men with guns tucked in their waist each carried a wooden box that opened at the top with a metal handle.

"How many?" asked the same man from the league.

"Three hundred twenty," answered one of the men holding a box. He could not see their faces from behind the stone pillar he was hiding in, but he could see this was a short man with the stomach of someone who frequently drunk alcohol. The man continued, "Thirty bottles are purple or black."

"Place them on the table," said one of the other men from the league. The three followed, putting down the boxes on the table.

"Which box?" asked the man with the pistol.

"Here," answered one of the three men, pointing at one of the boxes.

He opened the box, examining the contents. He then took out one bottle and peered at it against the light—it had black gel swirling inside it. Then, replacing the bottle into the box, he continued examining the other bottles. He then opened the other two boxes to look at the contents.

"Everything good, Norman?" asked one of the men.

The man with the pistol nodded his head. When he was satisfied inspecting the bottles, he closed the boxes and gestured at the other two men to take them, before he took and carried one himself.

"Tell Vern we need more black dreams next time," he said, before turning away.

He stayed still behind his hiding place, willing himself to be a statue and not breathe. Upon peering at the men who brought the boxes, he saw one of them took a black gym bag from under the table before leaving.

He stayed where he was until he heard the footsteps of the three men carrying the boxes fading, at which time he slowly crept out of his hiding place and followed in their direction, keeping himself in the shadows and attached to the walls.

The three men headed to a part of the headquarters he had never been to before, and they opened a metal door that led to another room.

"Oh, shoot," he quietly muttered to himself as he saw the door slowly closing behind the three men.

Just as the door was about to close shut, he ran as quietly as he could, quickly grabbing the handle just before the lock clicked close. He held his breath for a few seconds, looking around to make sure no one was there. And when he was sure he was the only one there, he slowly pulled the door open and slid behind it, quietly closing it afterwards.

He found himself in a room that looked like a warehouse, with a high ceiling and giant windows that were shut closed. It reminded him of the warehouse they raided during their second test. There were rows of huge cabinets containing wooden boxes, much like the boxes the three league members took.

They were on the other end of the room, peering at the boxes that were now open, and he looked around trying to find the glass case his brother mentioned. There was no glass there, it was all wood, all cabinets and boxes. He crept closer to the men, looking around to see if he could spot anything different, anything that would stand out to him.

"Twenty-six, twenty-seven, twenty-eight," one of the men was counting as he took the bottles of dark gel outside of the box and laid them on the table. "Twenty-nine, thirty. Right, just as Rowan said. Thirty bottles."

One of the men took a smaller box, and he started placing the dark bottles inside it. He watched, trying to see where the man would store the dark bottles—perhaps his answer would be there.

The man closed the box and handed it to the other man with a pistol slung on his shoulder, the one called Norman. As soon as he had the smaller box, he started walking towards the door. "Pack everything up," he said to the two men left behind. "And don't start consuming any of the dreams in that box; you know what happened last time."

He stayed right where he was, hidden behind one of the huge cabinets, and slowly followed Norman to the door. As soon as Norman disappeared behind it, he quietly grabbed the handle to keep it from completely closing, and then he took a few moments before he quietly opened it.

The hallway was empty, not a sound of footsteps to give him a clue whether Norman went left or right, both directions heading towards completely different areas of the headquarters. He slowly walked right, checking, but there was no clue there. He went the other direction, but no one was there, too.

For the next 15 minutes, he walked around trying to figure out where Norman headed and where he would take the 30 bottles of dark dreams, but his efforts were futile. He went back to his bed, feeling a sense of frustration.

"The Makus," it was Abe. He came to see him to tell him about the shipment and how he did not find where the dark dreams were brought. "Of course, they are here somewhere. Everyone was told we are trying to save Makus, but no one knew it was the league who created them in the first place."

"Created them how?" he asked.

"Unintentionally. A result of a botched experiment. They were supposed to be killed, but something happened and they got away, and out there they evolved into something else… Multiplied, and now, they are out of control. The league had been trying to capture every Maku, to protect everyone, but also to ensure their secret does not get out."

"Is there a way to save the Makus?" he asked.

"I don't know," Abe shook his head, deep in thought. "I have never met any Maku. I have only heard of them."

"I am going to see the Maku children who are here. Perhaps there is a way to help them," he shared. "And I need to find where the dark dreams are stored. I need to find Mom's dream."

"Be careful," said Abe. "The league will not hesitate to remove anything it sees as an obstacle to its plans. The sooner we find the dreams, the sooner we can get out of here," and then he added. "I have thought of several plans so many times before to help me disappear the moment I leave this place, and now I can start working on some of those plans for both of us. We must disappear into safety, at least for a time, before we decide what to do next and how to put a stop to the league. For now, just be careful."

"I will."

A few days later, he found himself following Peter and Chloey crawling through a vent in the ceiling. The twins had long found an entrance near their room, which allowed them to explore various areas of the headquarters unnoticed. One time, they found themselves in the room where the Makus were kept.

"Which other parts of the headquarters have you explored?" he asked in a low voice while following the kids on all fours. "Did you see where they stored dreams?"

"Just the areas in the lower level," Chloey, who was right before him, answered back in a whisper. "Sometimes we would watch everyone training in the hall from the ceiling, or see new recruits arrive and we would tell who would last and who wouldn't."

"We know where the weapons are stored," announced Peter in a voice louder than a whisper, which was quickly followed by a shush from Chloey.

"We know where they store the dreams," said Chloey. "But the vent doesn't lead there, just the hallway. We see them come and go, but we have not seen the dreams."

He did not answer, still wondering where the dark dreams were being kept.

Soon Peter stopped, and so did Chloey. They peered through an opening that led down to a room. Peter knocked three times on the ceiling before removing the cover.

"We brought someone," Peter announced, speaking to the room below them. "He wants to meet all of you. He is, our friend." And then he looked back at him and Chloey. "Come on."

Peter slowly lowered himself through the vent opening, and Alec could hear voices coming from below as they helped Peter. Next was Chloey. She lowered herself with ease that looked like she had been here and done this several times before.

He slowly crept towards the vent opening, and then he peered down to several faces looking up at him. He scanned the faces until he found the one face he was looking for—the Maku girl. As soon as the girl saw him, a mix of hatred and fear crept in her face.

"Why did you bring him here?" she asked Chloey, a tone of betrayal in her voice. "He was the one who hurt me."

"He's our friend, Mariel," Chloey explained. "And he's a good person. His name is Alec."

"I'm sorry about what happened," he said, looking down at everyone whose faces all registered suspicion. "I had to help my friend. You hurt her first."

"Your kind have always been hurting us, hunting us," an older boy, a little younger than him, spoke up with fire in his only eye. The boy had a long scar that ran across his right cheek, from the base of his nose to the upper right of his forehead. It crossed his right eye, which was no longer there. "We just want to live peaceful lives," the boy continued. "But you kill our parents, and then you take us here against our will and do all sorts of things to us."

"That's... That is not me," he explained. "I didn't know the truth about everything, and that's why I'm here. I want to know the truth, and I want to know how I can help you."

"He's not going to hurt you," it was Peter. "I promise. We are friends."

For a moment no one spoke a word; they all just stared at each other with suspicion. Until Chloey said, "Can he come down and speak to you? I promise he will not do anything bad."

The boy threw him a dirty look, before turning to Chloey and answering. "Fine. But only because you and Peter have always been good to us."

He slowly lowered himself down into a chair that was placed on a table right below the opening in the ceiling. And when he was finally down, he counted six Maku children in the room. The youngest was a small boy, even younger than the Maku girl named Mariel. The oldest was the one who spoke to him, whose name he learned was Zee. He also found out he had been the longest in captivity.

"They killed my parents," Zee revealed. "And my older sister. And then they brought me here about 5 years ago. I was the only one here for a while, before everyone was also brought in one by one."

"What do they do to you here?" he asked.

"They torture us," one boy answered. He was much younger, and he almost had no hair. What little left was there were all gray and white in color.

"Are they the one who did… That?" he pointed at the boy's hair, and then looked at Zee's scar. Looking around at the six children in the room, he could see something wrong with almost all of them.

Zee had the scar on his face, and the other boy had almost no hair. There were two other boys, and then the two girls. One of the boys had blisters on one of his arms, while the other boy looked okay but had a bandage around one of his hands. The two girls looked better, although one of the girls had bleeding on her lips. Mariel seemed okay, colors still dancing around her fingers. Every now and then, he would catch her looking at his own hands, at the colors dancing around them, too.

"They would take us into a room, one by one," said Zee. "And then they would force us to take dreams. Some of them were too much. One time when I was still the only one here and they forced a black dream into me, I didn't realize I had clawed at my face and my eyes trying to get the dream out of me, or to get out of the dream. I woke up all bloody."

"Do you know why they're doing all of these to you?" he asked.

"They said it is to cure us," the boy with a bandaged hand spoke, and there was anger in his voice. "But that's a lie. They would hurt us, and even if we tell them to stop, they don't. And they keep on killing us, we would move from place to place so they would not find us, but they still do."

"I overheard the Professor once," it was Zee. "They thought I was unconscious, but I wasn't. And I heard him talking about creating dreams that would bring a new start for everyone. They are trying to create dreams from us."

"Create dreams from you? Like... A human dream machine?" he furrowed his eyebrows in confusion. "How? Consuming others' dreams is prohibited because it is harmful to the mind, but creating a new dream out of someone—I have never heard of that. How is that possible?"

"I don't know," answered Zee. "I don't understand it—why we're here and what they plan to do with us. They would not give any answer whenever I try to ask."

"Can you help them get out of here?" it was Chloey who asked.

He was quiet, looking around at all the eyes that looked back at him.

"I... I do not know," he answered, uncertain. "But I will try and see what I can do."

Chapter 24

The thought stayed with him throughout the night and the following day—what he could do to save the Makus who were captive in the headquarters. It was the same thought in his mind when he left the dream room after a training session with the twins and Nicolas, when Gregory approached him in the hallway.

"This afternoon at 2:00 PM—come see me," he announced, and then left.

"See you? What for?" he asked, but Gregory had already turned away.

That afternoon, he knocked on the door to Gregory's room.

"Come in," he heard his voice answered, and he did. The man gestured at him to sit down, before announcing, "The Professor wants to see you."

"See me? What for?" he asked. In truth, he had been waiting for this. Abe told him the Professor would want to meet him soon, to know how he could be of use to him and the league given his capabilities for handling dreams.

"Real work," Gregory answered, looking at his hands. "You are no longer a recruit. You are officially a member of the league, and it is time to do what you came here for."

"What is that?" he asked.

"You will find out," Gregory answered, and then the man tapped him on the shoulders in a rare show of gentleness. "We all have each a role to play in fulfilling the league's vision of healing this world, and I know you will do great."

He looked at the man, wondering whether he knew the truth or, if like so many others in the league, he believed in its vision.

After a while, Gregory continued, almost as if musing to himself, "You and I, we're the lucky ones. We did not catch the curse that befell our generations, and I do not know why—why it must be you, or me, what we have done to deserve the gift we are given. But it must have been entrusted to us so that we can do what we can to change the world."

"The world," he said. "It's too big to change. There are a handful of us, and an entire generation of pale people. And the Makus, too. All living together in a hopeless world."

"It gets overwhelming, I know," answered Gregory. "The league started with one man's vision. And one thing we know so far, so many out there share visions that never saw the light of day, and only because no one was bold enough to stand out and claim that vision. But the league is here, and I believe in its vision. I am a part of it, and now you are, too."

"How do you know the league has the right vision?" he asked. "And that the cause you are part of is the right one?"

Gregory was silent for a moment. "I guess I don't know anything for certain, that is true," he conceded. "But we all must be part of something bigger than ourselves, live our lives for someone, something, outside of us, a greater cause, a higher purpose."

"And it's the league for you?"

"Yes. And it will be for you, too, now that you are here. Make it all meaningful, will you?"

He thought about what Gregory said, and what he knew so far about the league, wondered again whether Gregory was part of all of it, or if he was being fooled like everyone else. Finally, he said, "For the right cause, yes, as much as I know how."

The following morning, he followed Gregory to the Professor's quarters, in a part of the headquarters so hidden from anyone he thought he would not find it again even if he tried to. They went through a long series of tunnels, passed through several doors, dark and fully lit hallways, until he found themselves in front of a large door that opened into what looked like the size of another hall, like the one they trained in.

Inside the hall were machines of all shapes and sizes, some twice or thrice as big as he was. On one side of the room, there were several chairs with what looked like straps to hold people in, as well as a mechanical headgear fitted to whoever was strapped in there. They looked like electric chairs, and he felt a chill crawl through his spine at the sight.

There were a few people in white robe working around the vast hall, and no one that looked familiar to him—not Abe, nor Nicolas, though their robe looked like what the two would usually wear.

"What is this place?" he asked Gregory.

"This is where all the important things happen, the ones destined to make the most impact in the league's vision."

"And what is that?"

"Dreams!" he heard a booming voice announce from one end of the room, and he saw a man in a black suit and tie emerge from a small open door. For a quick second, he felt his chest tighten, as if his breath was squeezed out of him, at the sight of the open door. He could not see what was behind it, but at that instant he knew—the dream was there.

"Dreams—they are the future of this world!" The Professor walked towards him, followed by no other than Nicolas, who gave him a small, tight-lipped smile in acknowledgment. He noticed something different in the man, but he could not quite figure what it was.

"You must be Alec," the Professor offered his hand, and he shook it. "I have heard good things about you from Nicolas here," he tapped the small man on the back. "His stories speak of promise, and potential, and I could not wait to see it," there was a hint of excitement in the Professor's voice.

"What do you do here?" he asked. "And what are all these machines for?"

"These," he gestured around with open arms. "These will change the world, give us all a fresh start."

"Fresh start? How?"

"You know this world is cursed, right?" the man asked, walking around the hall, a tinge of sadness in his voice. "Our ancestors were a rich people. They could dream, and with that ability they could do everything. But alas, the treasures of the world became so tempting that they drew all their sights, all their desires, outward… Until what was inside was left untended; they have forgotten what really made it all possible—the soul, the heart… And anything that is untended, unnourished, it dies. And it was not long before we had a generation of people who were empty inside, unable to dream, devoid of color, living on what little was left in them."

"The pale generations, they call us," the man continued with his monologue. "And as the generations moved forward, we only got paler and paler. But you…" the man turned to him. "People like you and Gregory; you bring hope to this world. Because of you, there is a chance at redemption."

"Redemption?" he asked. "How can the league make that happen?"

"A fresh start," the man declared. "That is what we need." And then he gestured at him and at the seat with straps. "Come, sit, let us find out what is inside you."

"What?" he looked at Gregory, terrified.

"Go on," Gregory nodded to him in encouragement. "Nothing bad will happen to you, I promise."

He tentatively approached the chair, and Nicolas helped him to settle down on it. He was about to tie the straps on Alec's hands when The Professor stopped him. "Don't, no straps. If all that you told me were true, then he would not need the straps."

"Are you sure?" asked Nicolas. "He is just a kid. He might not have enough strength to handle it."

"Nah," the Professor shook his head. "You must start seeing potential, Nicolas, and start believing in it. We need to trust that the gifted ones, they can save the world."

He took two bottles from the pocket of his pants, a red dream and one that was purple but not purple—it had a translucent quality to it.

"What is that?" he asked, curious. He had never seen a dream like it.

The Professor smiled. "Let's see if you can find out. Open both of your palms."

He did. The Professor poured the red dream on his left palm, and then the translucent purple dream on his left."

"Professor," it was Gregory. "He will be able to handle this?" He wasn't sure, but he seemed to have detected a note of concern in the man's voice.

The Professor smiled. "Trust, Gregory. We need a lot of that if we are to build a new world. Unless we try, we will never know." Then he nodded at Nicolas, who lowered down the metal helmet on his head. It felt cool, despite his thick hair acting as cushion between his head and the metal interior.

"Close your fists and your eyes," Nicolas instructed, and he did. He heard a soft whirring sound that slowly grew louder and louder, until it was all that he could hear.

He found himself walking on a street that was almost deserted, save for a few people. It was a street lined by shops and stores on both sides. In front of one of the shops, an old man was sweeping the yard. He looked up, and there was a calm look on his face as he nodded to him and then resumed what he was doing. On another shop, a woman was pulling up the metal door that locked the shop for the night, revealing flowers of different colors and varieties behind the glass windows. And then on yet another shop, a man was wiping the glass windows with a wet cloth that he would dip in a bucket of soapy water.

"Good morning," the man greeted him as he passed by, waving his hand that was holding the wet cloth and splashing water everywhere.

He waved back. "Good morning."

When he turned a corner, the next street looked familiar—it was a street near their home, outside the gated community where they lived, only this time in place of the usual chaos and crowd and noise there was a peaceful silence.

There were men huddled around in front of a house, each holding a mug of what looked like steaming coffee. As he passed by, they all looked at him with bright and happy eyes—skin brown, eyes clear. And that was when he noticed it—no one had white streaks on their skin or their hair. Everyone he saw so far was normal. This wasn't the pale people. It was the same street, the same world, but… A new generation?

He looked around, and for the first time he felt the world open. A new day.

Then, he heard footsteps rushing towards him, and he turned. Something shifted around him, and the world that he felt opened just a few seconds ago seemed to have shifted, darkened, closed on him.

He saw a woman running towards him, a panicked look on her face. There was something wrong with the woman, but he couldn't put his hand on it. As she neared, he saw her eyes wide with fear.

"Hey," he called out, but the woman did not seem to hear him. She kept running.

When she was in front of him, he called again. "Hey!"

The woman was startled, and she stopped. She turned to look at him. For a quick second, a look of confusion registered on her face, but it was quickly replaced by panic and fear, and she grabbed his arms.

"Help me!" the woman said, almost with a croak.

From a distance, he heard more footsteps approaching, and instinct took over.

"Come on," he offered his hands to the woman, and she took it. The moment their hands touched, the world spun around him, and the next moment he found himself in a room that looked vaguely familiar to him, the woman still holding his hands, and she suddenly emitted a panicked shriek that made him jump.

He let go of the woman's hands, and he saw they were in a room with two people.

"Hector, please," the woman pleaded, addressing him.

He was confused. "What?" he asked, but no voice came out of him.

"I promise," the woman continued to speak, tears streaming down her face. "We'll find a way out of this. We'll find a cure. We just need time."

He found himself approaching the woman, who retreated away from him. And that's when he realized what was wrong with her—the black of her eyes kept changing colors, one moment black, and then green, and then purple.

"Please," she continued to plead. "Don't kill me."

"Kill you?" he asked. "Why would I do that?"

Again, no voice came out.

"Professor?" one of the two men addressed him, waiting for the next instruction.

He looked at the man, confused, and then he realized where he was. He looked around, and he saw he was in the headquarters—different, but the same.

"It's time, professor," he heard the man address him again, and he found himself nodding.

The two men moved in sync, taking the woman, each man half carrying and half dragging her by her arms.

"No!" she shouted, hysterical. "Hector, please! Don't kill me!"

"Wait!" he called out, but again no voice came. "Wait!" he repeated, this time with a loud shout, trying to get himself out. And finally, both the two men and the woman heard him, and they stopped. He approached the woman, who stopped crying. He stood in front of her, and when he looked behind him, he saw the Professor looking at them.

"Who are you?" he asked the woman.

"I am Agatha," she answered. "Please don't let them kill me."

"Take my hand," he said, and she did. The moment their hands touched, everything around him spun once more, but this time he held himself steady, looking at everything moving around. The next moment, he was back in the same street he was in before he encountered the woman. The first thing he saw was a looming structure at the end of the street.

He walked towards it, and as he got closer, he realized what it was… A wide gate, and behind it a grassy area, with stone crosses randomly scattered about. It was a cemetery. When he was right in front of the gate, he looked up to see what was written on the arc above the gate: "The Pale Generations."

He saw an old man walking on the other side of the gate, inside the cemetery, carrying a rake and a shovel.

"Hello," he called out. The man looked up and saw him, stopped, and stared at him for a moment, as if deciding whether he was seeing someone there or if he was just hallucinating. "Hello," he called out again. "Is the cemetery open?"

The man decided he was a real person and approached him, the rake and shovel still in each of his hands.

"You shouldn't be here," the old man said. "No one is allowed to enter the grounds."

"What is this place?" he asked.

"It's a cemetery, what else," the man said, sounding impatient at his question. "And no one is allowed in."

"Why not?" he asked. "Pale people cannot visit their dead?"

"What do you mean visit their dead?" the man asked. "This is a long-forgotten place, long closed and locked. This is where all the pale people ended. And who remembers them? No one."

"Wait… I don't understand. All the pale people have died? And everyone out here…"

"Not died," answered the man. "Killed. In the name of a new society, a new world."

"What?"

Suddenly he understood. He held into one of the metal bars of the gate, and the world around him started to dissolve, moving unsteadily like a gel. He could feel the soft texture on his palms as the metal bars he was holding onto also dissolved in his hands. He bent the bars, and he stepped inside the cemetery.

The old man started protesting, but he had lost his voice, and his form started to get distorted as everything around him melted into each other.

He walked unsteadily in the grass, which swayed with each step. The graves had no epitaphs, just blank stones that marked where each person was buried—no identity, all memory of them gone.

He took one more step, and then he felt all the air squeezed out of him, and he gasped as darkness closed around him. When he opened his eyes, he was still gasping for breath, and air seemed to have rushed inwards to his lungs, causing him to cough incessantly.

Chapter 25

"Are you okay?" Nicolas asked, taking the headgear off.

He blinked, and his environment became clearer and clearer with each blink. He looked around at Nicolas, and then the Professor. There was no one else there.

"Where's Gregory?" he asked.

"He left," answered Nicolas, taking a closer look at him to make sure he was okay.

That was when he noticed it, what was different with the man. The three-dotted tattoo he had looked different, raw. The dots were no longer of the same size; the two bottom dots were now bigger, like the one Gregory and all the other leaders had. He felt fear creep into his stomach as he remembered Abe and what those changes in Nicolas' tattoo meant for his brother.

"How did it go?" the Professor asked, approaching him, and looking at his right hand. He felt the soft gel in his hand, and then he realized there was nothing on his left hand. There were two dreams, and now there was just one.

He raised both of his hands and opened both palms. And indeed, his left hand was empty. On his right hand, there was a gel of a color he had never seen before. A translucent color that shifted from dark to purple to yellow, the colors constantly moving inside it, merging, and then separating from each other. And then he remembered the dreams.

"What are those dreams?" he asked, trying to piece everything together in his head.

"What did you see?" the Professor asked, holding a small clear bottle towards him. He extended his palm and poured the gel into the bottle. The Professor gazed at it with a look in his eyes that Alec could not explain—a mixture of delight and awe, and what looked like a hint of madness.

"A street, almost deserted," he answered. "Everyone looked… Not pale."

"Ah," the Professor smiled. "The shopkeeper sweeping in front of his store?"

He nodded. "Yes, and someone opening her flower shop. A man cleaning glass windows and waving at me."

The Professor continued to smile. "One of my most favorite dreams. It was the dream that started all these."

"But the woman," Alec continued. "That one wasn't a dream, was it? It was a memory. That is why the gel was different, translucent."

The man's expression turned grim, and he grew silent.

"She was a Maku, wasn't she?" he asked. "I could see the changing colors in her eyes. One moment she was there, and the next moment gone. Did you kill her?"

The man did not speak for a moment, but then after a while he said, "Every dream has a trade-off. We all must do our part."

"But killing?" he asked. "No dream is worth another person's life."

The man stared at him, first with wonder, and then it was replaced with something else—a look that a father would patiently give a child who was trying to understand something but failing.

"One life, or a few," the Professor said, his gaze growing distant. "To usher in a new society, a new world. That is worth every price."

"Who was she, Professor?" he asked, remembering the terror in the woman's eyes. "She called you Hector. She must be someone close to you."

The Professor blinked a few times, as if trying to erase the memory in his mind. And then he asked him, "What else did you see?"

He thought about the woman one more time, and then he remembered the old man.

"A cemetery at the end of the street," he answered. "Where the entire pale generation was buried."

The Professor's eyes widened, the corners of his lips turning up and his eyes lighting up with a crazed look.

"Everyone dead?!" he asked, his smile turning into a creepy grin. "Are you sure?"

"There was a man, a groundskeeper," he answered, trying to remember. "He said it was where all the pale people ended, and that it was a forgotten place, locked forever. It was filled with unmarked graves, no names, or any form of identity."

"Yes, yes!" the Professor exclaimed, more to himself than to anyone in the room. "Just as I envisioned! It all paid off!"

"What paid off?" he asked, suspicious.

The Professor looked at him, and again that look of wonder took over his eyes.

"You," the Professor took his hands and looked at them. "I cannot see the colors in your hands, but I know they are there. And I know you are special, just like Nicolas and Gregory said. We can rebuild this world together."

"Wait," he said. "I don't understand. What was it that I saw?"

"Don't you understand?" the Professor said. "You saw the future. And it was always as I imagined it to be."

"The future?" his mouth hung open at the thought, a gnawing terror growing at the pit of his stomach. "It wasn't a dream, or a memory?"

"No," the Professor answered, raising the bottle with the new dream. "It's this. You saw a memory, and a dream, and then you saw the future. How special!"

"The future? With the entire pale generation killed? Is that what the league is all about—eliminating the pale people?"

The Professor turned to him, and this time there was a hard look in his eyes. "The league is all about building a new world, a new future for all of us. And the only way to do that is without the pale people."

He felt dizzy, his head spinning. The Professor continued.

"You see, the world is sick. And if we don't do anything, everything in it will turn dark and rotten. Consider the body being attacked by a virus, invaded. The way to heal it is to kill the virus. And the way to heal the world is to rid it of the pale generations—start anew. And now we have seen, that is possible."

"How do you plan to do that?" he asked.

"These," the Professor gestured at the room, at all the equipment around him. "We know people are not all bad, but sometimes the bad parts are simply too much that the good parts are not enough to redeem them. The pale generations are like that, too. They are not all bad, but they are beyond redemption."

"However," the Professor continued. "We do not want the good parts to go to waste, and that is why we have all this equipment. The new world will need all the good parts, and it deserves that."

"But the pale generations, they are people, too," Alec protested.

"Of course they are," the Professor said. "But every dream has a trade-off, remember? And this is that trade-off. We cannot save the pale people. Believe me, we tried—but they are beyond saving. So, in the name of a new world, they must go. But even if they must, they will be glad to know that they can contribute to building this new world—with whatever dream, whatever memory, they have in them."

"Wait…" the terror in his stomach grew at the realization. "These machines… These are to harvest dreams and memory from the pale people?"

"Trade-off and sacrifice," the Professor repeated. "These dreams and memories will form part of the foundation by which the new world will be built. It will be the legacy of the pale generation, and they will be remembered for it, not for the rottenness that grows inside them day by day. Isn't that a better use of life?"

"So…" he found it hard to continue to speak. "So… This is what the league is all about? The reason the league exists?"

"Dreams are the reason the league exists—their preservation, and the preservation of the world. And you," the Professor turned to him. "You are born to take part in that. That is what your gifts are for."

The elimination of an entire generation, he thought, feeling the chill creeping up his spine.

"Come with me," the Professor gestured at him to follow. He did, feeling dizzy and unsteady on his feet. The man headed towards the door leading to the other room, and the moment he opened the door Alec felt the same thing he did the first time he saw it open when the Professor emerged earlier. His breath quickened and his chest tightened, and he felt himself being pulled inside.

The dream!

He followed the Professor, and as he entered the room he was overwhelmed by different sensations. He smelt sweet flowers, the same fragrance that always lingered in his grandparents' home when he would visit them so many years back—they had a garden filled with violets.

And then, he felt the taste of baked cookies in his mouth, and he was transported back to his childhood when his mother would bake walnut cookies every Sunday afternoon, the recipe of which had been in their family for decades, passed down from one grandmother to another.

Memories came rushing at him, and random images flashed in his mind, some of which foreign to him, and yet they felt familiar—a wedding and doves flying, mornings at the beach, and a teacher holding a pointing stick that he would point at a blackboard, with children's voices echoing all around him as they read the words on the board together.

"Come here," the Professor called out, and the barrage of memories stopped. He found himself in a room filled with glass cases, each one containing more bottles. The bottles were different, though—either darker or more translucent.

Placed on a metal table was a metal safe, and the Professor was opening it. His heartbeat quickened at the sight, and he just knew at that moment—the dream that was stolen from them and caused his parents' life was there.

The safe opened, and there were several bottles of dreams inside it, even more different from the rest inside the glass cases in the room. His eye caught it— his mother's dream. It was the reddest of red, and the only one of that color not just in the safe but in that entire room of special dreams.

The Professor took out a bottle that was so dark it looked almost darker than black, and he held it to the light.

"These are the most prized dreams in our world, blood and sweat," he declared, almost wistfully. "These will give new life to our almost dead world, and we can begin again."

"How?" he asked, not sure if he really wanted to hear more.

"Dreams are the most powerful elements in the world—their disappearance has proven that. But while dreams have doomed our world, they are also going to save it."

The Professor replaced the bottle and locked the safe, before continuing, "The pale generations, we cannot save. But those that we can, we will. People like you, people in the league, we are given the mission to rebuild this world, and sadly we will have to cleanse it before rebuilding can happen. We had a hiccup with some of the machines and the things we are doing, but Nicolas is here and has been helpful in keeping us on track—and we are ready. And now, we want you to be part of this."

He looked at Nicolas, who remained silent but gave him a small nod.

"We will create a better world," the Professor said, a tone of confident certainty in his voice.

Chapter 26

"I know where the dream is," he told Abe the next time he came to see him. "But we must hurry. The Professor mentioned everything is ready, with Nicolas helping keep everything on track as they planned. I think Nicolas is going to replace you."

"Of course," Abe shook his head. "I have always suspected they brought Nicolas in for all of it. I tried to delay everything when I discovered what it was all about, but they started suspecting I was trying to thwart their plans."

"I can take and steal the dreams back now that I know where they are. I just need to find the key in the Professor's quarters," he said. "But we need to destroy those machines, and they looked indestructible."

"I helped create most of those machines," Abe said. "I can destroy them."

And then he added, "Romulus is going to help us once we leave this place."

"Romulus? He knows about you being in the league?"

Abe shook his head. "No. He had always denied the league's existence, but I found out about it through Mikos and Lara," he said, referring to the Gatherers.

"Why didn't you tell him?" he asked.

"He had always been suspicious of the two; he didn't trust them. And so, I was sure he would not want me to join the league," Abe said, and then added. "But he knew I did. I guess he had always suspected that I ended up joining when I stopped working for him. And the first note he sent me when I reached out to him was a question asking whether you found me."

Alec grew thoughtful, remembering the old man with the burnt fingers.

"We need to find a way to get into those machines and destroy them," Abe brought him back to the task they had at hand.

And then he remembered overhearing a conversation between the Professor and Nicolas while he was in the room with them. "The Professor will be away for two days next week," he said. "It will be the perfect time to put our plans into motion."

"Next week," Abe pondered. "That will give us enough time to complete our preparations. We destroy the machines, we take the dreams, and then we leave this place. Without the machines, the league has nothing. And then we can expose it."

Alec nodded, thinking of the days ahead of them.

The next time he was back in the dream room, it was with Peter and Chloey. They had started working on dreams under the guidance of Nicolas. After the time he spent with the Professor, Nicolas asked him not to tell the twins anything.

"They are not ready," he said. "They need time to just hone their skills before they get involved in league business."

He agreed, thinking it would be best, too, to protect them from the league.

"Okay, your turn," said Nicolas, addressing the twins. He had just finished with a memory exercise and came out of the room slightly dizzy. Nicolas had been helping him navigate through memories. While he had a good handle of dreams, he would always feel unsteady after emerging from a memory. He did well during the time with the Professor, but continuous exposure to memory seemed to have caused problems with his balance.

"As for you," Nicolas turned to him. "Stay here for a while, rest and recover."

He nodded, and Nicolas headed to the next room with the twins in tow.

The moment the door closed shut, his eyes went straight to the table being used by Nicolas, and he quietly walked towards it. Nicolas was a neat guy. Everything in his desk was placed in proper order. He scanned the desk, reminding himself not to misplace or mishandle anything. Nicolas would probably notice anything that was out of place.

He slowly opened the drawer, making sure he did not make even a small squeaking sound. As expected, everything had a rightful place in the drawer. He was looking for a key, a tube-like key in a red ring holder, as Abe described it. It was the key that would safely unlock the ankle monitor that bound his feet without alerting anybody.

It was not in the first drawer, so he opened the next one, and then the next. In the third drawer, he found it, a small cylindrical key held by a red ring holder. He took it and placed it in his pocket, and then he carefully closed the drawer. And just as the drawer was about to close shut, something caught his eye, and he took and examined it. There was no mistaking, he had seen this before—it was the key to the metal safe in the Professor's quarters. What were the odds? He took the key, too, and closed the drawer quietly. After double checking that he had not misplaced anything in the desk, he went back to the chair he was sitting on to take some rest while waiting for the twins.

"Okay, see you next time, kids," it was Nicolas' voice, and he opened his eyes. He realized he had dozed off while waiting for the twins to finish, and when he woke up the three were back in the room.

"Are you feeling better?" Nicolas turned to ask him.

He nodded. "Yes, much better."

"Okay, good," he said. "I will see you all three tomorrow."

At that, the man went back to the other room, as the three of them also shuffled out of the dream room. As soon as they were out of the room and were far away from it, Chloey gestured at him to stoop down so she could tell her something. He knelt in front of the twins.

"What is it?"

"You should take us with you," Chloey said in a whisper.

"And the Makus," added Peter, more loudly.

"Sssshh!" Chloey placed her index finger to her lips, gesturing at her brother to be quiet.

"What are you talking about?" he asked, suspicion growing in his mind.

"We know about your plans," Peter said in a lower voice. "We heard you talking to Abe."

"Talking to Abe?" he tried hard to keep his voice calm. "How did you know that? And does anyone else know about this?"

"No, no," Chloey reassured her. "Just us. We saw you sneak to the dream room once, so we sneaked in the dream room, too, through the vents."

He had almost forgotten about the vents. Of course. But if the twins had known their plans, how easy would it be for Nicolas, or even the Professor, to find out?

Chloey probably noticed the worry and hesitation in his eyes, and she touched his face. "I promise we won't tell, but we don't want to stay here after you leave."

"We didn't know the league is bad," it was Peter. "If we had known, we wouldn't have come with them when they recruited us."

"Are you sure no one else knows about this?" he asked. "Did you tell your Maku friends?"

"No, we did not," Peter assured him. "Only Chloey and I know about your plans."

"But please take us with you," begged Chloey. "And our friends. We promise to help."

He was silent for a moment, thinking.

"Okay, let me talk to Abe and see what I can do," he relented. "But promise me you will not tell anybody about this. This is dangerous. If anyone finds out, we never know what the league will do—our lives will be in danger."

"We promise," Chloey said.

Peter raised his right hand. "Cross our heart and swear to die if we tell."

He laughed, trying to quell the worry he was feeling, and then ruffled the boy's hair.

"I will let you know when I have talked to Abe. For now, just act normal, okay?"

Both boy and girl nodded.

Chapter 27

Abe had been hesitant about the plan to take the twins and all six Maku kids with them, but after some discussions and convincing from him, he finally relented and made the plans for all 10 of them to escape. Before long, the appointed day had come, and he found himself anxious but ready.

He would help Abe escape using the key he took from the drawer of Nicolas. They would go to the Professor's room—it would be empty at the time with the Professor away. He left the previous day and was coming back the following day. While there, Peter and Chloey would lead the Makus out of their room through the vents. They agreed to meet by the entrance in the forest, where a truck would be parked and waiting for them. They would escape to the dessert, and someone—a friend of Abe—would be waiting to pick them up. If everything happened according to plan, they would be far away by the time the Professor returned.

It was late in the night as he quietly slipped into the dream room, finding it empty, with only a few lights on. As usual, he went to Abe's room and found him waiting.

"No one saw you?" Abe asked, a strain evident in his voice.

"No one," he answered, taking the key from his pocket, and handing it to Abe, who took it and began deactivating the monitor around his ankle.

"And the kids?" Abe asked.

"Peter and Chloey should be coming to get them in the next hour," he answered. "We will meet them outside in two hours."

The metal gear around Abe's leg clicked as it was finally deactivated and unlocked, and Abe carefully placed it on the floor. He took a briefcase containing all the things he took from the room—files and blueprints of all the things he had work on and had been working on until present, each one a piece of evidence pointing to the league's plan.

"Let's go," he said, slowly going out of the room and into the dream room. It remained empty, as it should be at this late hour.

He went straight to the door and slowly, quietly opened it, looking left and right to ensure that the corridors remained empty. And when he had ascertained that it was, he motioned for Abe to follow him.

With light feet and carefully measured steps, they walked-ran down the hallway and trudged through the long series of tunnels and pathways that led to the Professor's room. After what seemed like eternity, they finally found themselves in front of the door.

It was Abe's turn to produce a key from his pocket, and he effortlessly unlocked the door with the said key.

"Where did you find that?" he asked.

Abe gave him a mischievous smile. "From a long time ago, when I was still in the Professor's good graces. I had a hunch there would come a time when I would need this key, so I took it. And I was right."

They quietly slipped through the door and into the room, and the wide hall managed to inspire his awe a second time. The gigantic machines looked indestructible—how did they expect to break those machines?

"What's your plan?" he asked Abe. "These looked like they were built to be impenetrable."

"You forgot that I designed almost all of these," Abe gazed at all the machines around and before them, his eyes sporting a mixed look of fondness and pride. "I know their weak points and their limitations. I know exactly how to break them and render them unusable."

He approached one of the machines, a cylindrical glass the size of a regular basketball and connected to a bed with several metal tubes attached to it. Abe gazed at it, almost with longing. And then clenching his jaws, he went to the main keypad that operated the machine. He pressed on a series of buttons, and the machine started coming to life.

"What are you doing?" he asked, staring at the lights that started to illuminate inside and around the machine.

"Do you know what this machine is and what it is designed to do?" Abe asked, and then continued with the work he started. "This is a Memorsum, a machine I designed for extracting memory out of a dream. It was found that at the core of every dream, there is a memory. If we can extract that, we can explore the essence of every dream, and that will open the door to so many possibilities."

"The bed—what is it for?"

"Dreams, our body naturally expels them," Abe answered without looking up. The lights in the machine started turning from blue, to yellow, to orange. "But memories, our brain closely holds on to them. And when we dream and the dream is expelled from our body, the memory is left behind. Have you ever wondered why we sometimes dream of the same thing repeatedly? That is because the memory that is its essence—it remains in us, always there."

The lights have all turned orange, and one by one, they started turning red, and an alarm started to sound off. He watched, mesmerized at the sight. Until suddenly, everything was red and the room was filled with an incessant ringing of the alarm, reaching a crescendo that ended into a smoke erupting inside the glass cylinder. The next moment, the red lights were gone and the machine looked dead and quiet.

Abe stepped back to look at the machine one last time, and for a second a momentary look of regret crossed his face, before he squared his jaw and turned to him.

"One machine down," he said, before turning to the next one. And remembering something, he turned to Abe, saying. "You should get the bottles of dreams. And pack them carefully."

He nodded, remembering the backpack that was slung on his shoulders. He made it to the other room, and the moment he opened the door he was besieged by the same emotions he felt the first time he met the Professor. A barrage of sensations came rushing at him—the smell of violets, baked walnut cookies teasing his taste buds, his mother's voice as she talked to him while he was still in the womb.

"You are Alexander, from your great grandfather," he heard her say. "And you are so very loved."

He felt the voice enveloped him in a feeling of safety and peace.

"Come here, Abe," he heard his mother say. "Come meet your brother. Say hi. This is Alec."

He felt his brother's small hands touch him as he touched their mother's round belly. "Hi Alec, I'm your big brother."

His heartbeat quickened, and his eyes automatically went to the metal safe that was on the table.

He strode to the table to check and found the safe locked, as he expected. He took the key from his pocket and inserted it into the keyhole. The moment the safe opened, it was there—the reddest dream of them all. He took it and held it to the light, and for the first time he saw that it had a translucent quality to it, like the dream the Professor gave him the first time. He looked at it intently, wondering if it was more than just a dream, and then he heard his mother say in his head, "Thank you for finding it. It is now yours."

He took a few deep breaths, allowing his mother's voice to linger in the air, before he heard her saying in a rush, "Quick! They are coming!"

He was pulled back from reminiscing, and an intense feeling of panic overcame him. "They are coming!"

He opened his backpack and the boxes inside it and took the bottles from the safe, carefully but quickly packing them. When the safe was empty, he took more dreams from the cabinets and packed them, too. He remembered what Abe said—they would not be able to pack and take everything, but they must take those in the safe and whatever else they could.

Once the backpack was full, he zipped it and quickly went out of the room, the feeling of panic rising in his chest.

"We have to hurry; they're coming!" he shouted to Abe as he ran back to the other room, only to find Abe was not alone. The Professor was there, together with Nicolas, Gregory, and Victor.

Chapter 28

Everyone turned to him as he entered the room.

The Professor had a seething look on his face, which turned to a look of confusion upon seeing him.

"Alec? You, too? You were part of this?" there was disbelief in the Professor's voice.

"What are you doing here, boy?!" Gregory's voice thundered around the room.

He looked at Abe, who had a look of defeat in his eyes.

"He's not part of this," Abe exclaimed, trying to save him. "This was all my plan, and I tricked him into helping me."

Everyone looked back at him again.

"Well?" the Professor asked. "Speak!"

A series of loud knocks at the door interrupted the conversation. Nicolas went to open it, and several guards came in, bringing with them five of the Maku children.

"We found them huddled outside, trying to get away," announced one of the guards. He looked at all five kids in horror, but they had no fear in their faces. What they all had was a defiant look, as they stood straight and refused to cower.

The Professor turned to Abe. "This was you, too?" His voice was hard with anger.

Abe did not speak, merely looked at the Professor with clenched jaw.

The Professor turned back to the guards in exasperation. "Where is the other kid?"

"We're trying to find her as we speak," the young man answered, a tinge of nervousness in his voice.

"What's the plan here, Abraham?" the Professor turned back to Abe. "Your attempt at being a hero, it will be your death, and you know it. There is no stopping what is to happen—the old world must be destroyed if we are to bring in the new world."

"You cannot wipe out an entire generation," Abe said. "It cannot be the beginning of a new world."

"This is not the first time it's happening," the Professor countered. "We've had entire species gone in the past, obliterated by some natural force. Nature created them, and nature wiped them out. This time, it was man who brought forth the pale generations into the world—by our greed and materialism. It is up to us to wipe them out and start a new world."

"That will not happen," declared Abe, trying to sound courageous and trying to mask the small waver that was in his voice.

The Professor laughed a hollow laugh. "And how do you plan to stop me? Alec here," the Professor turned to him. "He had seen it, the future. Why don't you tell him, Alec? What you had seen—the pale generations gone, buried into oblivion... And a new world springing forth to replace it. A renewal."

"The cost to make that happen..." Alec shook. "You killed that woman, didn't you? The one in your memory. Who was she? Was she your wife, sister, friend? She trusted you, and you killed her."

The Professor's face darkened at this. "We all have sacrifices to make to bring our vision to reality. It was a sacrifice I chose to make—and it is going to be worth it."

"Aaaah!" From out of the corner of his eye, he saw Zee run towards the Professor. In a quick and sudden movement, the Maku boy took out a knife from his waistband and aimed it at the old man. Before he could reach him, however, a gunshot rang in the air and the boy stumbled and fell, blood oozing from the back of his head. It was Victor who fired the shot.

"Nooo!" the Maku children shouted and cried as they ran towards the fallen boy.

Meanwhile, out of instinct, Gregory snatched the gun from Hector. "What are you doing, man?! It's just a kid!"

The Professor, looking visibly shaken, tried to compose himself. "Take the Makus and strap them to the chairs!" he gestured at the chairs lined up along one corner, the same ones in which Alec laid down during that very first time he met the Professor and he discovered that memories could be extracted, too.

The guards followed, taking the crying children, and strapping them on the chairs.

"Now go!" the Professor ordered. "Find the other Maku girl and bring her here!"

The guards shuffled out of the room. And Nicolas, who had been inspecting the machines, announced, "Most of the machines have been destroyed."

The Professor threw Abe an angry look, before turning back to Nicolas. "Will you be able to repair them? Get them operational?"

"It will take some time," Nicolas answered. "But I can."

"Good. And you," he turned to Abe. "I have actually thought I saw potential in you, a hunger to prove your worth, and I thought you could lead with me in the future world, but I guess I was wrong."

"I would not be a part of your future world," Abe spat. "Not with the way you want to build it."

"So be it," said the Professor, a finality in his voice. "Perhaps you have no place in that world, after all. Hector," he gestured at the combat leader, who understood.

Hector seized Abe and strapped him in the one remaining chair, together with the Maku kids. He placed the metal helmet on his head.

"Professor," it was Gregory. "Don't do this. We need Abe."

The Professor retrieved a bottle from his pocket, and Alec saw its translucent purple content. It was the mixture he created when he ingested the Professor's dream and memory and saw his vision realized. The old man gave Gregory a quick glance. "We don't need him. Why do you think Nicolas is here?"

The Professor approached Abe, who was strapped to the chair. "I will make you see what it's all supposed to be, even if you won't be here to see the vision realized."

"No," Alec rushed towards Abe, but Nicolas was quick to restrain him. "His mind won't be able to handle it!" he shouted.

The Professor threw him a malevolent smile. "That's the plan."

"Don't do this, Professor," Gregory approached Abe. "There must be another way. Abraham is an asset."

"Don't take another step," Victor held a gun at Gregory. "Or believe me, I will shoot you."

Gregory raised his hands. "Don't do this. He is one of our own."

"Not anymore," the Professor said, pushing a button on the chair and then placing the content of the bottle on Abe's palm, closing the palm firmly with his own hand.

The machine whirred, and Abe looked at him.

"No, no!" Alec shouted, unable to free himself from the grip of Nicolas.

Slowly, Abe's gaze began to assume a glassy look. "Abe! Abe!" he shouted. "Remember mom! And dad! Keep your focus on my voice!"

The Professor glanced back at him with a small look of surprise.

"Ah, of course," he said. "You're the lost brother. Tsk, tsk," he shook his head. "Too bad. You two, you could have a good future in the league."

He didn't hear much of what the Professor said. His eyes were locked on Abe, who had his eyes wide open, lost in another world.

"Stop!" He suddenly heard a familiar voice, followed by a loud thud.

They all turned to the voice, finding Peter who jumped from the vent in the ceiling, followed by Chloey, and then Mariel.

"What are you doing here?" the Professor asked, his eyes turning to Mariel. "Ah, there you are, the guards have been looking for you. Your friends are also looking for you here—it is time you join them."

Mariel looked at the Professor with eyes blazing, and Alec saw the color in her hands turning dark red.

"No! No!" Abe shouted, and Alec watched in horror as his brother writhed on the chair, veins bulging on his face.

"Stop it!" he shouted at the Professor, trying to free himself from Nicolas' grasp.

Out of the corner of his eyes, he saw Gregory move. And in a split second, he was grappling with Victor, trying to take the gun out of his hands.

"Aaaah!" Mariel came running towards the Professor, her hands blazing. However, before she could reach him, Nicolas jumped on her path and pushed her away. The girl looked startled as her small body slumped on the side, no match for Nicolas' strength.

"Don't hurt my friend!" shouted Chloey. "Peter! Now!"

Peter threw sand in the air, followed by a small amount of gel colored dark green. The next moment, sand and gel merged and it was everywhere, all around them. Peter and Chloey flicked their fingers and the sand and gel mixture moved towards Nicolas, surrounding, and enveloping him.

"What is this?" Nicolas asked, his voice muffled by the mixture surrounding him. The next moment, the mixture wrapped around him, sticking to his skin and suffocating the man. He fell to the ground with eyes open and his mouth wide, frozen as he uttered his last words—shouts of "No!"—before completely losing consciousness.

Mariel took the opportunity and turned back towards the Professor, who retreated from her.

"Don't you dare touch me, you dirty Maku!" he hissed at the girl, who continued to advance towards him.

In the middle of all the commotion, Alec ran towards his brother, who was still strapped on the chair, writhing in agony.

"Abe! Abe!" he called out. "It's me, Alec! Listen to my voice!" Abe continued writhing, not hearing him.

As he called out to his brother, a gunshot echoed in the room, and Victor fell on the ground, clutching his bloody stomach where he was hit. Gregory kicked the gun away and got up, looking around the room in time to see Mariel clutching at the Professor's wrist. The Professor was lying on the floor shaking, his eyes wide but unseeing.

"Stop! Stop!" he shouted, but Mariel was also lost in her own world, and soon the smell of burning skin permeated the air in the room and smoke rose from the Professor's wrist as Mariel tightly held it, unable to control herself. The Professor's body convulsed one last time, and then he laid flat and frozen on the floor, his chest unmoving.

Meanwhile, Peter and Chloey were huddled with Alec as he tried to call out to his brother.

"Listen to my voice," Abe desperately called out. "You can get out of there!"

For a moment, Abe stilled, a momentary clarity crossing his eyes, and they all watched with hope and anticipation. But his body gave one last convulsion before falling back on the chair, all energy gone.

Chapter 29

"No! No!" Alec cried out. "You can't leave me alone! You can't!"

He shook his brother's body, but there was no response. He noticed everyone surrounding him; Gregory had unstrapped the Maku children from the chairs. Chloey and Peter were crying, while Gregory, trying to comfort him but finding no words, simply tapped him on the shoulders. The rest of the Maku kids were quiet.

He got up, trying to think what to do next, when he felt the backpack still slung on his back. He didn't realize he still had it, with all the bottles of dreams inside. And then he remembered.

He quickly unslung the backpack, carefully placed it on the floor, and opened it, finding the bottles neatly arranged in boxes inside. He shuffled through the first box until he found it—the reddest dream he had ever seen. He took the bottle and sat down beside Abe, and then he looked at everyone around him.

"I will try to bring him back," he said, hoping against hope it would work.

He then uncapped the bottle, poured the gel inside it on his left palm, and he held Abe's wrist with his right.

Instantly, he was overcome by a warm feeling that settled on the top of his head, travelled down to his face, his neck, shoulders, back, chest, arms, and hands, and down his thighs, legs, and feet. When he was fully enveloped in a sensation of red warmth and safety, he opened his eyes and looked around, and he saw himself in front of a house he had never seen before but strangely felt familiar.

He was in the front porch, and on his left, he saw a young girl playing with dolls—a man and a woman. He approached her, watching the colors that were dancing around her hands as she moved them.

"Hi," the female doll said to the male doll, the girl moving the female doll's hand to wave at the male doll. "Welcome to our world."

"Hi there," Abe said to the girl, and simultaneously the girl said the same thing, the male doll's response to the greetings of the female doll.

"I have many beautiful things to show you here," said the female doll to the male doll. "My name is Abigail. What's yours?"

Upon hearing the name, Abe looked closely at the girl, and he started to see the familiar features. She looked so fragile, so far from the strong woman he knew that was her mom.

"My name is Abraham," the male doll's response to the female doll. "It's nice to meet you."

Alec smiled at discovering his brother's name came from way, way back, and he couldn't take his eyes off the girl. He was suddenly overcome by an intense longing for his mom.

"It's nice to meet you, too," Abigail said, and he suddenly looked at Alec as if she was seeing him. "Come inside—I have so many things to show you."

And then the girl, abandoning the two dolls, ran inside the house. Alec followed, and when he came in, he felt different—he felt an excitement and giddiness that he could not explain.

"Mom! Dad!" he heard himself say, and he was startled by the voice that came out—it was that of a girl.

A younger man and woman were coming down the stairs, and both beamed at him when he saw him.

"Abigail!" the man exclaimed, picking him up and raising him above his head. He realized he was in his mother's memory, and the man and woman were his grandparents.

"Did you find anything exciting outside?" his young grandmother asked, smiling, and he recognized the same smile in his older grandmother back in his childhood before she died.

"I found a ladybug," he heard himself say in his mother's little girl voice. "It was beautiful. I watched it but did not touch it."

"Very good," his grandmother said. "Your dad has a surprise for you."

"What is it!?" he excitedly asked.

His grandfather gently put him down and took out a glass bottle from his pocket. He recognized the content, a red gel. The young man then knelt in front of him to show him the bottle up close.

"This is from my own grandma, whom she inherited from his father, my great grandpa. This is his dream. My grandma passed it on to my dad, and your grandpa passed it on to me, too," the young man explained, fondness evident in his voice. "Someday, I will pass it on to you."

"It is a dream?" he asked in a girly voice.

"Yes, but not just a dream," his grandfather explained. "We found that as it was passed on, memories were passed on with it, too, so now it contains not only dreams from your ancestors who loved you but also their memories."

His grandfather stroked his cheeks. "When I pass it on to you, it will have some of my memories, too, and then some of yours when you pass it on to one of your children someday."

He took the bottle from his grandfather and held it carefully in his small, girl's hands, looking at the gel inside. Even then, the red gel had taken on some translucent quality.

"It is beautiful," he heard his mother's voice.

"It is," his grandpa said. "And someday you will have it."

He held the glass against the light, and the gel shone for a few seconds, the glare causing him to close his eyes. When he opened them again, he found himself in a hospital hallway.

He looked around, trying to find something familiar and trying to feel everything around him to ascertain whether he was himself or whether he was in someone else's memory. He felt like his old self, and this he confirmed when he looked at a nearby mirror and saw himself in it.

Where am I? he thought.

As he looked around, he saw a nurse approaching. He was pushing someone on a wheelchair, and upon closer look he discovered it to be his mom, carrying a baby in her arms. His younger dad was following them behind closely, holding several papers—hospital files.

They went into a nearby room, and he followed. Inside, his dad took the baby while the nurse assisted his mom to the bed.

"Hello," his dad was smiling at the baby, greeting him while he held him in his arms. "Your name is Abe, Abraham. And I am your dad, Henry."

Her mom was settled on the bed, and she looked at father and son fondly. "You two are adorable."

Henry brought Abe to Abigail, and he peered at his brother. He looked tiny, innocent, his eyes peacefully closed.

"How do you feel?" Henry asked his mom, caressing her hair and kissing her on the forehead.

"Better, now that you're here, though a little tired," she smiled at him.

"Rest," Henry took Abe from her arms and placed him on the smaller bed beside Abigail's bed. He then tucked Abigail so she could sleep and rest.

He approached his older brother, who opened his eyes when he felt him nearby. The baby looked at him and smiled.

"Hi," he greeted, smiling back at his brother, unsure whether the baby could see him. "I'm your younger brother."

The baby reached out his hand, and he moved closer to touch his tiny fingers. He felt something in his pocket, and immediately he knew what it was, and why he was there.

He took the bottle from his pocket, and the gel inside glowed red. Is it safe for his brother, a baby? He had to try. He had to trust the dream and the memories in it.

He touched Abe's tiny hand and softly opened his palm, pouring the red gel on it and closing the palm back.

The smile disappeared from Abe's young face as his eyes turned glassy, and Alec held his breath, feeling a mixture of fear and anticipation in his chest. And then, Abe's lips curled up and his smile was back, and before long he was laughing and giggling as he wiggled his arms and kicked his legs.

"Come back," he whispered to the happy baby. "Come back to me, brother. I need you."

After a couple of minutes, Abe settled down and closed his eyes peacefully, and the red gel was back in his palm. Alec poured it back on the glass bottle and closed it, before placing it in his pocket. He then looked at the peacefully sleeping baby, his chest rising and falling steadily. He took the baby's hands, and then everything blurred and he felt a steady warmth embracing him.

When he opened his eyes, he was back in the Professor's room with everyone surrounding him.

"Are you okay?" it was Gregory who asked.

He felt a little dizzy, but everything felt fine and right. He nodded, "Yes."

He then looked at Abe, and the gel was in his palm. It had now a translucent red orange hue. He poured it back into the bottle and waited.

"Abe," he whispered. "Come back."

For a few moments Abe did not move, but then he inhaled deeply as if filling his lungs with all the air around them. The next moment, he opened his eyes and fell into a coughing fit.

He helped him sit down, until the coughing subsided and he had calmed down. He looked around at each one of them, and then his look settled on him.

"You were there," he said, eyes wide as he remembered everything. "It was all beautiful."

He raised the bottle, and Abe stared at it. "This was…?"

He nodded, grinning. "It is now yours. I passed it on to you."

"What?" he looked confused. "But that's from mom, that's…"

"Yes. I know," he did not let him finish. "This is family heirloom, and you are my family."

He handed the bottle to Abe, who took it, stared at it, and then hugged him tight. "Thank you. And thank you for saving me."

"And they lived happily ever after!" It was Chloey who declared, approaching, and hugging both. The kids all crowded around them, hugging, while Gregory looked on with a smile on his face.

"Not yet," Abe declared afterwards. "We still have work to do."

"Are you destroying the rest of the machines?" he asked.

"No," Abe answered. "I deactivated them all temporarily, but we may have yet some good use for them in the future. The right use," he stressed. "But for now, we are at least assured the threat is gone."

Abe turned to Gregory. "Thank you. I have always had a good feeling about you."

Gregory approached and shook Abe's hand. "Some of the other leaders have started to question the recent decisions of the Professor, suspecting something was wrong about the league and its operations," he said. "They will be interested to know about the truth and about what happened here."

Abe then turned to him. "We may not have to hide, after all."

He hugged his brother once more. "I'm just glad you're back."

"Me too," said Abe.

"Let me talk to the leaders," said Gregory. "It's time to clean up the league."

Chapter 30

The training hall had its usual chaos that morning—dream hunters practicing and new recruits training.

"Alec!" it was Carl, practicing swords with a recruit. "We're going hunting tomorrow! Want to come with us?"

"Yes, of course!" he shouted back. "I have a new pair of daggers—I need to put them to good use!"

Carl grinned, and then he gave Abe a nod before continuing with the practice.

"It's good to be free again," Abe said, a look of renewed energy evident in his steps. "It's been a long while since I last walked these halls.

Since that fateful day when they finally put a stop to the Professor and his plans, the league had taken on a new energy, one that was more open and more accepting of the world around them.

"Abe!" It was Gregory, walking fast towards them. Even he looked more relaxed than he was before. "Can you come with us this afternoon? We are visiting another Maku settlement. This one, we have never had contact with before, but they heard about what has been going on recently, and their leaders reached out to meet with us."

They had started making progress reaching out to the Maku communities, establishing connection, and assuring the leaders the league would no longer hunt them, that they could now work towards building their communities and coexisting in peace.

It turned out that despite the abnormalities they suffered in the hands of the Professor, or perhaps because of it, what the Makus lost were replaced by something extraordinary, much like the gifts Abe and some of them have. And in repairing their relationship with the Makus, they found new ways to work together to improve their respective communities.

"Of course, I will go with you," answered Abe.

They both had since developed a deep respect for Gregory, who now led the warriors in the league. He, on the other hand, would replace and take the place of the Scientist as they continued to oversee the dreams in their care. Chloey and Peter would be his apprentice, and their first mission was to return all the stolen dreams to their rightful owners. Meanwhile, Abe started working to get the machines in proper order and was now entrusted with leading the redesign of the vision that would determine the future and role of the league in their community from here on.

"And Alec," Gregory turned to him. "I talked to Karim. His mom had agreed for him to join us."

"Karim is finally joining us?" he asked, excitement in his voice. He told Chloey and Peter about the boy, and they were both excited to meet him.

"Yes," Gregory answered, before turning away.

"Things are changing for good," he said to Abe. "And I have a good feeling about the next few weeks and months."

"I do, too," Abe said, relishing in the flurry of activity around them. Things were about to change for The League of the Dream Hunters.

ACKNOWLEDGMENTS

The leap I made from short stories to novel was not easy, but one I have always known I wanted to make. At one point, I wasn't sure this novel would see the light of day.

I thank God that it did, and I owe deep gratitude to the people I have journeyed with and those who have supported me throughout the writing of this novel.

My biggest thanks goes to the Scribblory Writers Group, who has always been my writing family since the first day I found it, and to Scribblory founder Ms. Elaine Marie Factor. I wouldn't have been here without the community. Special thanks, as well, to Scribblorists regularly attending the Scribbling Hour sessions, with whom I have shared my journey in writing this book.

Thank you to Ukiyoto Publishing, for opening new doors for writers and aspiring writers like me.

The Dream Book Project that is a collaboration between Scribblory and Ukiyoto gave me the positive push I needed to help me keep working on the story despite the struggles and self doubt. I am sincerely grateful to the writers who have been my classmates in this project and who are also publishing their books and sharing them to the world. Congratulations!

To my family and friends–thank you, as always, for your outstanding support and encouragement as I pursue my love for the craft of writing.

To the writers and aspiring writers from the communities I am a part of and who are a part of my writing journey one way or another, thank you for continuing to share the energy and the inspiration.

And to God, the ultimate Writer of my life, thank you for the gift of life and for the gift of writing. I continue to entrust all my words, all my stories to you—from you, through you, for you.

About the Author

Naysan Albaytar

Naysan Albaytar is a Bicolana who grew up in a small farming community. Her childhood was spent before the era of the internet, and it was one she spent outdoors, among the woods and in the garden in their home. It was in these places where she first discovered the wonders of her imagination. The garden became her "market" when she was playing house and needed produce for her imaginary cooking. The woods became worlds of adventure in her young mind. It is this same imagination that she now goes back to whenever she writes new stories, brings to life new worlds and characters on the pages of her notebook or laptop.

Writing and stories have always been a key part of her life. She started with writing essays in school so many years back, followed by a stint in the high school paper. In college, she continued to practice the craft of writing when she pursued a degree in secondary teaching, major in English. And after college, she went straight into a writing career.

Naysan continues to write today. She has published two books during the past few years: a memoir entitled *Remembering Pandan, A Farmer's Life and Other Stories* and a short story collection entitled *All the Light Around Us*. She is a communications professional and a freelance writer, and she is also a Scribblory writing mentor.

You may reach out to Naysan via the following:

EMAIL: nice.albaytar@gmail.com

FACEBOOK: In the Footsteps of the Sun

IG: In the Footsteps of the Sun

www.ingramcontent.com/pod-product-compliance
Lightning Source LLC
LaVergne TN
LVHW091632070526
838199LV00044B/1030